Southern Discomfort

Heather Daughtridge

Aberdeen Bay

Harbin - Washington, D.C. - San Diego

Aberdeen Bay
Published by Aberdeen Bay, an imprint of Champion Writers.
www.aberdeenbay.com

PUBLISHER'S NOTE

Aberdeen Bay is not responsible for the accuracy of this book--
including but not limited to events, people, dates, and locations.

International Standard Book Number
ISBN-13: 978-1-60830-080-8
ISBN-10: 1-60830-080-3

Printed in the United States of America.

Acknowledgements

When I first began writing this book, I owed many thanks to my trusty ten year-old coffee pot. My journey quickly became a family adventure. Over a period of two years, my family not only put up with my late-night and weekend writing, but they encouraged me every step of the way. They allowed me to hold it near and dear to my heart until I was ready to share my characters. To my loving husband, Will, and my two precious children, William and Meredith, this book is for all of you. My extreme gratitude and love extend to Mom, Dad and Mimi for listening to and encouraging my dreams. To Mary Margaret and Dwight, thank you for checking on me and making sure I was still actively writing. To two lifelong friends, Lynne Conklin and Karen Anderson Wood, thank you for putting up with me for decades and helping shape who I am today. I owe huge thanks to Lynne Lewis, my Raleigh editor and new friend, who took on my project and made it better with each turn of the page. Jennifer, friend and owner of Jennifer Robertson Photography, makes me smile both in front and away from the camera. Ross Murphy, a million thanks for believing in this book and me. A special acknowledgement goes to my late great-grandfather, Joseph Tunnell, for his beautiful poetry that is incorporated throughout this book. To all of the people who have touched my life, I am more appreciative than you'll ever know. Finally, to my two late grandmothers, Ada and Nellie, I am forever grateful for your love, wisdom, grace, and the wonderful content you gave me for this book!

Chapter 1

Mrs. Ruth, Gran's best friend and community Avon peddler, waited until seven in the morning to call our house. Immediately recognizing the number, I knew why she was calling. I had been dreading this call for months. Without pause, I did what I do best; organize everyone around me. Within the hour, the four of us began the three hour journey to Fairfield, Gran's home for more than ninety years.

Until today, my painfully normal life has mirrored scenes from the movie *Groundhog Day* for as long as I can remember. Since giving birth to the stereotypical one boy and one girl "perfect life" child pattern, my morning routine has been as predictable as the squelching North Carolina summer humidity. Matt, my better half for nearly twenty years, has mastered the timing of his morning departure from the bedroom to coincide with the three of us almost out the door; and like clockwork, looking stunned when there is nothing left for him to do to help us get our day started. Without fail, the next scene of our day with Stella's and Graham's morning banter of "I beat you to the sink" and "I have a better snack than you" echoed in the oh-so-typical blue minivan complete with stale fries under the seat. The only reprieve in my predictable script of routine was that the yuppie minivan could operate on autopilot if the coffee I relentlessly nursed turned out to be decaffeinated.

My life's *Groundhog Day* episode used to end the same every night by talking to my treasured grandmother, Gran. Almost deaf and blind from her cataracts, Gran knew when I was smiling but hiding disappointment or hurt. Her gift was the ability to sift through my muddled words to detect the fear in my voice when I was scared that the new fall couture line would not be profitable. Gran would know that my exhausted voice after nursing sick children also held gratitude that I had kids to hold tight. Gran made my life complete.

But today is different and tomorrow will be, too. Even though the morning banter will continue and our daily routine will be a peaceful chaos, I can no longer view what was my neatly packaged life in the same way again.

~

Everyone knew Gran. From the county commissioner to the waitress at Harris' Restaurant, Gran was known to the tight-knit coastal North Carolina community of Fairfield as Ada Grace. Her name fit well in a family with other names like Nellie, Mildred, Iberia, and Myra. Thankfully, those deeply-rooted Southern names had skipped right over me. Gran outlived many of her family members and friends, but that did not stop her from making new relationships with people much younger. Gran's energy and stamina kept her moving alongside the seventy year-old book club members well into the evening.

The barren fields and gray landscape look extra cold on our drive to Fairfield. Matt keeps a steady pace on the two-lane roads even though we are slowed by several tractors easing carefully down the road. Inside, the car is unusually quiet except for the occasional groan from Scarlet, our treasured family pet. We round the last big curve after Piney Woods and I get nervous realizing Fairfield is next on the horizon. In recent years I was more of an observer around town. Today, however, I feel confident the community is waiting for our arrival as we are the main participants.

Passing through town as a mourner instead of a visitor is heart wrenching, especially past the church where Gran spent most of her life and I spent hundreds of Sundays. She inhabited the small Hyde County community for more than nine decades trying to feel big by telling people what to do, what to say and how to live. While hearing the latest gossip at breakfast bingo, she was planning her next meal for the shut-in who lived up the lake. Her multi-tasking bossiness included a real understanding and love for those around her regardless of age, economic status, and most importantly, race. Fairfield was her home except for one three month hiatus to our home in Raleigh. Ironically, leaving her home nearly killed her. After eight weeks of being cared for night and day, Gran tenderly asked could she go home to Fairfield. Knowing she wouldn't receive adequate nursing care, Matt and I were extremely hesitant to send her back to live in what seemed to be desolation. After a few days of listening and watching her, I knew the right thing for Gran was to go back to Fairfield. Even with poor health care in her final weeks of life, she was back at home and that was where her heart lived.

We meander down the country roads to the hunting lodge, our home for the next few days. For the first time in over thirty years,

I am thankful that nothing has changed in the area for decades. The lodge has been standing for nearly one hundred fifty years, still sturdy and strong, just like Gran right up to her final days.

The lodge, nestled next to a towering elm tree, seems almost small under the blanket of limbs that have been part of the landscape even longer than the structure. Over two hundred acres of rich, black soil surround the lodge on three sides. The soil could probably be sold for the same price as gold since anything planted in it would flourish without question. The farm now tended by a large farming outfit from the Outer Banks, used to be lovingly cared for by family. I grew up watching Gran, Papa and their farm hand, Kurt, plant corn, soybeans, and raise thousands of hogs. Each summer, I gave up hairspray and makeup to become "one" with the pigs. The tireless daily ritual of filth and grime was priceless to my being. Now, the hog and sow houses stand tattered and torn with no signs of life.

Kurt, a short, stocky, sweet-faced black man, had been more than the farm hand – he was part of the family. Mrs. Junie, Kurt's wife since the two were fifteen, made the lodge home to dozens of hunters and fishermen who came from near and far. Keeping visitors in line was easy as she would quietly threaten to cease making homemade biscuits, fresh apple cobbler and ice box cookies. Each morning, Mrs. Junie rose before dawn, filling the house with rich aromas which equated to love. Hymns from the Baptist church filled the kitchen as she prepared meals that satisfied both hearts and appetites.

Kurt often referred to me as "him." It was not inconceivable as most people shortened my name, Samantha, to Sam, a name typically reserved for boys. I can reluctantly admit that my hair definitely contributed to the confusion as it was a shoddy version of Princess Diana's coveted 1980's hairstyle. With all of these factors facing Kurt, he was certainly not to blame for the confusion during my awkward preteen years.

As a young child, I sensed early on that the relationship between my grandparents, Mrs. Junie and Kurt was built on respect. They allowed one another to be who they were and intertwined their lives while building trust, dependency, and love. Even as a young child I perceived this as refreshingly unusual since they surpassed generational and rural community prejudices.

~

The front door to the lodge creaks as if it hasn't stirred in years, which is probably true since Kurt died nearly seven years ago. He used to take care of all that needed mending around the farm, lodge and Gran's home. Although she was as tough as the oyster shells that lined the driveway, Gran relied on Kurt to help her keep things running. When he passed away three years after Papa, a piece of Gran's heart went with him.

The dark, cold, and musty smell confirms this as it is obvious that human touch had been missing for a long time from this treasured home. I watch as Matt and the kids fill the lodge with our belongings and within moments we have officially taken over the space. Scarlet sniffs every nook and cranny and eventually trots off with a prized find below the dusty floor-length drapes.

Even though Graham spent several weekends at the lodge as a young child, he examines the layout and walks in and out of each room several times. Knowing him very well, I can see that he's starting to relax once he gets his bearings. Stella flutters through the downstairs as if she's floating. Sure that she is running on adrenaline, a collapse is sure to happen by late afternoon.

Matt lays out our clothes. Luckily, I had begun preparing for her death the moment Gran left Raleigh. Even though I had many black dresses, I bought a special one that has no memories attached to it. Stella's presence during the moments before leaving for the church is God-given with her illuminating life and energy. Beaming like a light of hope while twirling in her black velvet dress, she halts suddenly, stops in the middle of the floor and says, "Mommy, I feel like a princess today in this dress. Do you think Gran would like it?" Stella takes my hand and rested it on the soft velvet.

"Baby, Gran would be so proud of you and think you are beautiful." I struggle to whisper the words while stroking the fabric making different patterns.

Almost eight years old, Stella has always been our special gift. When Graham was only thirteen months old and I had just started spending more hours at *je t'aime*, we found out we were pregnant for the second time. It was a busy month preparing for the spring fashion show as my business was just beginning to grow. Not wanting to wait for Matt to retrieve several large boxes from the storage closet, my stubbornness kicked into overdrive and I took over the task myself. Trying to move the task along, I decided to lift the three boxes at once. As I felt the top box starting to topple, it was too late for me to try and catch my footing. With an unbalanced first trimester physique, I backed up into another stack of storage bins and went straight down with the three large boxes collapsing one by one on my protruding belly. Stunned for several minutes, I did not move a muscle until I felt something moist in my maternity pants. Assuming I had leaked a bit of urine with the impact, I wasn't immediately concerned.

After I wiggled from underneath the boxes and made my way to the bathroom, I quickly noticed blood splotches on the floor. This was it. My biggest fear had come true. We lost a baby that day, but more importantly, I lost a piece of my soul. Matt never once blamed me for the accident, but deep down I knew if I had waited for him to help me, we would have avoided this tragedy altogether and our baby would not have died.

Gran had true empathy as she drove to Raleigh to be by my side after I was released from the hospital. Although we rarely broached the subject, I knew she and Papa had lost a child many years ago. Experiencing grief after not even having held the baby we lost, I couldn't imagine their pain of losing a child that they had watched grow and loved for years. Gran's only advice was to give Graham a sibling. Matt and I tried to be intimate again after I was cleared by the doctor, but I physically and emotionally could not put myself there again for almost a year. One evening in the middle of the night, Matt awakened me from a deep sleep. I had fallen asleep on the sofa as I often did after an exhausting day physically and emotionally. It was obvious Matt had been tossing and turning for hours. Taking my cheeks in his hands, he said in the quietest voice I had ever heard, "Sam, I do not blame you for your fall. I only wish you would allow people to help you like I was going to do that day with the boxes. I am telling you that you need to let me help you now. Let me show you that I love you with all of my heart and that life can go on."

With the most careful moves, Matt and I made love for the first time in months. As we reconnected physically, we bridged emotional gaps that were screaming to be healed. Nine months later, our Stella was born. We had our baby girl and Graham had a sibling. Most importantly, we were moving forward.

Those remembrances seem like a spec in my memory.Graham, almost eleven, looks like a young man as he stands hesitantly in the doorway looking awkward in his dark suit, but very handsome. His dark hair and athletic build make him look like a young man, something I am not ready to face at this moment. Graham has always been an "old soul" understanding bits and pieces of life that some people would never be able to grasp. He and I share a special bond that is unspoken, but felt in the inner core of my being.

~

The five mile drive to the church seemed to take less than a minute. I was paralyzed in the car with years of memories rushing over me like a wave of emotions. All I could picture was the church yard green and lush during Homecoming, the pinnacle event each summer. Every year the church was transformed with large tents filled with fried chicken, fresh vegetables, artery clogging coconut cake, pies, pound cakes, and every kind of salad you can imagine. Even with tropical storm force winds, Homecoming prevailed.

Baptisms, weddings, and funerals evoke similar feelings of indescribable emotion in this century-old church. There is never a dry eye while experiencing the passing of life, the union of two people, and the blessing of a new baby. Even the sun-weathered farmer with his towering stature and broad shoulders that protect his six children is visibly moved in this church.

The small but commanding structure is a spectacle with its woodwork detail and stained glass. Whether the church is filled with cut flowers from the ditch banks or the local florist shop, fragrances are prolific in the intimate setting, especially in the summer without air conditioning.

Large cardboard fans with some type of religious emblem, usually a white Jesus figure with long brown flowing hair, are always readily available in the pews. Gran sounded like a broken record lecturing me that it's not "becoming" for a woman to perspire. For years, I did not know the word perspire was synonymous with sweat, but my intuition kicked in and I realized it must not be becoming for a young lady to "sweat" either.

Without delay, people sense which behaviors are allowed and which are forbidden within ten minutes of stepping through the large mahogany doors. The tolerable list embraces fan waving, lip syncing to a hymn, and wiping a tear when Blessed Assurance is sung. The big "over my dead body" list undoubtedly includes using the visitor cards for doodling, chewing gum, and the biggest of all - silly giggles. I always feared getting tickled in church – the pew would shake like leaves on a tree and Gran would mouth "Samantha Lynne" and give me the "look." It took only one raised eyebrow to scare my shoulders stiff.

However, today, the beautifully stoic church would have a different meaning as I would be sitting in the front pew, not because I arrived to the church early for Sunday service, but because I would be mourning one of the people closest to my heart.

~

We take long and deliberate steps into the church to pay our final respects to Gran. The church feels different today. It's as if it there is an undefined line drawn between black and white, and I know Gran would not approve. The "colored" people, as Gran called them, were part of the community to her and many were as close as family. Without even a nudge from me, Matt quietly finds Junie and escorts her to sit with us. Now the service can begin.

Staying focused on the front of the church and the entry of the pall bearers, I hear people climbing the balcony steps and realize we must be nearing capacity. Even though the church is filled with loved ones, I realize our immediate family is small in numbers. Gran's presence always felt large at the many funerals and weddings that have taken place in the historic Methodist church, which made me never question that it was just the two of us after Papa died.

Since the age of eleven, Gran served as my sole caregiver as my parents chose to pursue their passion for Missionary work. In the beginning, they thought the assignment would last six months, top. After a year-and-a-half, my parents called Gran to announce that I would be joining them in Belarus. After about ten seconds of hearing my parents' proposal, Gran eloquently told them that she would not speak of the rubbish any longer; I would be staying with her in Fairfield. Gran would struggle with me living north of the Mason-Dixon Line, much less in another continent. Communication with my parents became sporadic; months turned into years except for the occasional quarterly postcard. With my parents unable to leave their post in Belarus, I am thankful that I can truly mourn the person who became my cherished parent.

The three person choir sings Gran's favorite hymns and the notes resonate beautifully throughout the walls of the church. I know, without a doubt, that surely the presence of the Lord is in this place. The rays of the sun filter perfectly through the stained glass directly above the altar. I look over at Stella who is lost in a trance sketching the lamb and waterfall from the glass on the back of the memorial program. As Graham begins to elbow Stella to stop her doodling activity, he decides to help her with the picture. He then writes a message at the top of the scribbled scene that says, "Great Gran, we will miss you forever." He quietly folds the program and places it in his suit pocket. Stella smiles at him as if she knows exactly what he is doing.

Longtime friend and minister, Bryan Stevens, delivers a beautiful eulogy that captures both Gran's wit and her stubbornness to never settle for less. He chuckles when recounting the story of announcing the contemporary worship service to the congregation. The younger generation embraced the idea of an interactive service with open arms. The older generation, especially Gran, thought that drums in a service were one step away from dancing with the Devil and fought the idea with folded arms. Within three services, Gran was among the first people to arrive to the contemporary service and could be seen tapping her toes to the rock and roll hymns.

Members of the congregation chuckle and nod their heads in agreement as many of them witnessed the story. Gran would accept the giggles in church today since the laughter was on her account. Desperately wanting the service not to end, but dying to be somewhere other than Gran's funeral, it concludes with the stately and sturdy casket being slowly carried through double wood doors. We follow methodically behind, passing into the next chapter of life. The feeling of finality is overwhelming. I will never see her face again. I won't hear her on the other end of the phone when I need a familiar voice. When I want to hear the truth but with compassion, I can't pick up the phone and dial her. When I am unsure of what tomorrow will bring, I can't call her to hear her faith that everything will work out. When Raleigh swallows me whole with all the hustle and bustle, escaping to Gran's warm and peaceful home will never be an option.

The ride to the burial plot is only a quarter mile down the road, but it feels like miles away. Traffic is never an issue in Fairfield, but the four cars that are on the road pull over to the side as a sign of respect. I feel nauseated as we turn onto the dirt path and meander our way to the tent and chairs that are waiting for us in this final step.

Not sure if it is due to the howling wind or the heaviness of the moment, Stella climbs in my lap and Graham curls up under my arm. It seems as though I am shielding them from the cold wind, but in fact, they are shielding my heart.

At the graveside, I choose to read my great-grandfather's poetry. Years ago, Gran compiled her father's prose and published a few of his works. It had been a treasure to her and was now becoming one for me. Saying the beautiful words is extremely tough for me, but I take my time reading "Continuing on My Journey." I taste each word that I speak.

> *The afternoon of life surrounds me*
> *And the beauty of life is blown;*
> *Now is the time I should look forward*
> *To the things I call my own.*

> *Dreams of the future on earth are about ended;*
> *It is time plans for eternity were built.*
> *Most of my earthly plans the years have settled,*
> *Only a few more to be fulfilled.*

In the prime of my life, in the morning
It was charged with constant force;
I saw so much that was needed
It held me on my course.

Most of the tools I have used on my journey
I have put aside to stay;
I will not use them anymore,
For I am nearly all the way.

Most of my comrades have made the trip And are waiting on the
other side.
Soon I will be there with them
Evermore to abide.

Most of the way the Lord has been my compass
And the Holy Spirit my guide;
But the devil's certainly been after me,
But I will not let him ride.

Now the sunset of life is very low,
Almost gone beyond the western hill;
Soon the stars of eternity will be shining
And I will be singing, "Peace be still."

There is not a dry eye, not even mine. Stella tiptoes over to the lectern where I am standing and wipes my tears with a linen handkerchief. I look down at the hand-stitched treasure and realize Gran had stitched a pink "S" in the corner surrounded by yellow and blue flowers. Stella kept it tucked away in her hope chest but brought it out when playing dress-up. After playing with it for a few minutes, Stella would lovingly fold and place it back for safe keeping. My heart is touched as I realize she packed it in remembrance of Gran. Out of the corner of my eye I see Graham remove the program with the drawing and note. Without a word, he takes my hand in his and we both place the kids' remembrance with the handkerchief. It seems only proper for the treasures to be laid on top of the mahogany casket sheathed by dozens of red roses.

This is the final goodbye to the strongest woman I have ever known. As people meander their way back to the fellowship hall, I stand stiffly as I watch the local men lower the casket into the grave. Gran is now nestled between Papa and Helen, the daughter they lost in an accident. My parents' religious dedication unfortunately did not rub off on me, but at this moment, I have no doubt in my faith and the ever after as my heart fills with peace.

Chapter 2

After saying goodbye to the two hundred plus people who came to honor Gran, I return to the worn-out lodge after a long day of paying respects to the woman I'll never forget. Matt drove Stella and Graham back after dinner to get settled from the exhausting day. Every great aunt, long lost cousin, and neighbor who either sold Avon to Gran or played bingo with her had squeezed the kids' cheeks and planted a wet kiss right on their faces. By the end of the long day, the kids had definitely heard enough of "you look just like your mom." Of course, Matt got zero percent of credit for their beautiful eyes and freckled cheeks.

As I approach the porch and take in a whiff of the faint pine smell, Matt greets me at the door with a mug in each hand.

"Hey there. I thought about having a glass of Riesling waiting for you, but I retreated to the safe choice of coffee." Matt's comforting tone is a welcome end to my day.

A smile comes over my face when I see our good ole' coffee supplies that Matt must have packed. Being self-professed coffee snobs, we grind our own fair trade beans which have to be a distinct bold flavor. Being insistent upon which part of the world the beans are grown, we dislike the weak stuff. It makes sense that when we travel, our fifteen year-old Gloria Jean's coffee grinder and Michael Graves coffee pot travel, too.

"I'm glad to be back here with you guys." I meant every word of it, too. Hearing the fire crackle in the den, I make my way to the comforts of the couch.

The kids are sleeping soundly in the bunk beds upstairs, leaving an eerie silence in the house except for the wind rustling in the adjacent fields and the occasional final drips of the freshly brewed coffee. Matt and I sit facing one another on the old green couch we brought to the farmhouse after making our last move to Raleigh. We couldn't imagine giving it away due to the little secret that it's where Graham was conceived. This is a memory that was BC (before children). It symbolizes the hope that once again we will be able to make love somewhere other than the bedroom.

~

   We fight our exhaustion and recap the day with stories of the who, when, what and where episodes that eventually piece together the fragmented day. The highlight of the day had been watching dozens of kids break free from the pomp and circumstance to play a raucous game of hide and seek outside the fellowship hall.
   After the burial I was relieved to have some time with my best friend, Carrie, who had driven from Raleigh for the day. It felt so good not to put on a fake face for a few minutes and to truly relax. Carrie and I were chatting with my oldest cousin, Bill, when he recalled a hysterical scene with Gran from our wedding. Regal in her aquamarine chiffon dress with pearl beading, Gran was perched in the center of the stunning Oriental rug singing "Wild Irish Rose" with all of her heart and soul. She had taken the spotlight in the 12x12 side parlor with a glass of champagne in one hand and my fingers in her other. After a series of the most classical works by Chopin and Schuster, it seemed only fitting to Gran that she shake things up a bit.
   Carrie chimed in sharing another memory I had forgotten, or conveniently had tried to forget. Without omitting any detail, she recounts the story of us waiting in the bride's chamber at First Presbyterian Church with Thomas, the minister, to have a few moments to gather our thoughts before my wedding ceremony. Gran sauntered into the parlor as if we were waiting for her and sat in the red tapestry wing back chair next to me. With a gentle hand, she stroked the white silk of my dress and proudly whispered, "I knew you would wear white to your wedding." Without blinking, she proceeded to say how pleased she was that Matt would be marrying a virgin. No one in the room moved a muscle. We just imprinted that memory in our minds, and it had obviously run deep as one of Carrie's funniest moments ever. As for Thomas, he had been an integral part of my time as a counselor at Duke's Talent Identification Program (TIP). His wink to us said it all as Gran got up from the stately chair, hugged me, being careful not to disturb the veil, and gracefully glided out of the room.
   Gran was on Thomas' case from the beginning as he forgot to sign the marriage certificate three weeks into the almost "sham" wedding, as she called it. Getting antsy, Gran called me to say that if Thomas didn't hurry up and get to the County courthouse, she would drive him there because it was not proper for us to be consummating a marriage that wasn't yet "on the books." Little did she know that we lived together in sin for almost a year before walking down the

aisle. This tiny little secret saved me from getting the talk of "that's not the way you were raised and good girls don't do that." I am sure that Gran expressed true relief on the day that I officially became Mrs. Samantha London.

Recounting that day's events actually recharges my batteries. Since the moment Gran died, Matt and I had not had a lot of time together with all the madness. We finish our last cup of coffee with a piece of pecan pie from the mounds of food lovingly prepared by the Fairfield Book Club group. Even though my pant buttons are bursting from the day's abundance, the homemade treats not only fill my stomach, but also heal the hollow place in my heart. My eyes close easily due to pure exhaustion as well as the need to escape the day's events.

Chapter 3

The morning hour peeks through the Carolina blue sky to the sound of geese honking in the distance and coffee perking. Matt had woken early to take Scarlet, the fourteen year-old fifty-five pound Heinz 57 mix, for a walk. Scarlet's entry into our household had been a reaction to our feeling that we needed to practice being parents before having kids. We foolishly equated having a dog as equal to the demands of raising children. I giggle as I realize the inaccuracy of this thought.

With a comforting cup of coffee in one hand and a small book in the other, I begin the morning in a weathered rocking chair on the front porch. Needing to feel connected to Gran this morning, I take my great grandfather's scarcely bound book, "A Collection of Poems," and curl up in the rickety chair. Over the years excerpts had been retold at various family gatherings and have become a family treasure. Gran was quite the wordsmith herself, commemorating almost any event into rhythmic prose.

As I read the dozens of poems, it was easy to picture Joe, my great grandfather, sitting on his front porch putting into words what he was afraid to say out loud. In the evening when the night was still and his seven children were finally asleep, I imagine him huddled near the fire trying to capture the last bit of light while writing his final words of the day. The time spent reading offers a deeper understanding for the magical words as they jump off the page into my heart.

The sounds of Stella's screams as Graham shoots every inch of her body with Nerf darts quickly catapults me back to the present. Stella slips on the dewy grass and lands face first in the black-as-tar dirt. Graham pauses for half a second and then pounds her back with six continuous Nerf strikes. Scarlet runs for cover under the elm tree's low limbs and within seconds, my solitude is gone.

After devouring breakfast sausage casserole, ham biscuits and cheesy grits, Matt, Stella and Graham pack up for the trek back home to Raleigh. My task at hand is to stay behind with Scarlet to get life wrapped up in Fairfield before my busy season cranks up at *je t'aime.*

    Je t'aime will be a perfect distraction for me when I get back to Raleigh. The passion which runs deep inside me for gorgeous fashion and fabrics, paired with being a people pleaser, makes me a natural fit for the bridal industry. Carrie is explicitly trusted to fill in during times I cannot be at the store, and this is one of the times I know I need to be in Hyde County.

    Watching the minivan drive away feels surreal as my role has always been to coordinate everyone's lives and routines. Intellectually I know they will all make it until my return to Raleigh, but I can't help pausing when I think about how their routine will be altered the next few days. This will be good for Matt and maybe even good for me.

    Matt's last words before driving away rang true. "You need this time to focus on Gran's house and belongings. Take the time without guilt so you can focus on whatever may be coming next."

    Scarlet and I collapse on the front porch listening to the silence except for the wind and the passing of an occasional car. Solitude feels foreign to me and I am unsettled by it, frankly. For years, I have been "on" twenty-four hours a day; however, I wouldn't dare change the demands on my time with the kids and motherly responsibilities. As I mature, I realize the choice is mine to be available to everyone. If I can't be there for my kids, I do not want anyone else to be there.

    Scarlet stretches with a dramatic yawn and settles into a nap. Ready for a nap, too, I realize I am utterly exhausted, both mentally and physically. Before settling down, I hover in the kitchen where Gran cooked hundreds of casseroles and desserts. It's the same kitchen where she entertained hunters and their families for years, the kitchen where she watched the men drink and say way too much. The kitchen now seems empty to me, even with all the food from the day before.

    Thinking I'd rest for twenty minutes with a power nap, I am startled by my cell phone ringing, and race to find it buried between sweet rolls and ham biscuits. On the other end of the phone is Carrie, who was running *je t'aime* until my return. Assuming something is wrong, I answer in panic mode.

    "Is it the Edwards wedding? Did the seamstress screw up the alterations for the Bynum wedding? Did the Jolly bride change the number of bridesmaids again?"

    "Sam, chill!"

    "Sorry, you know how I always assume something's wrong."

    "I know!That is not why I am calling. In fact, I need you to do something for me."

    "Sure, what?"

    "Now that you're starting to relax, take a deep breath and

walk to the hallway coat closet."

"What have you done?" I say as I follow her strict marching orders.

"You will find a Trader Joe's bag. You cannot, I repeat cannot, open it until later this evening. I know you, Samantha Lynne, and you have to wait until you're done with your day." Carrie says sounding almost mother-like.

"But Carrie, how did this get here?" I ask with a stutter.

"I paid Graham and Stella five dollars to put it there," she says with a twinkle in her voice.

Knowing I am on the right track, she says she has to go and "tend to new brides."

Overcome by appreciation at her kindness and thoughtfulness, I barely am able to mutter a whispered, "Thank you."

I make a promise to myself to wait and open the bag. In order to resist the temptation, I decide it's time to get my act together and head to Gran's house. The task at hand is to clean out closets, trunks, drawers, and whatever else calls my attention. The reward will be opening and viewing the contents of the Trader Joe's bag in the evening. After a slow start to the day, Scarlet and I are finally headed down the lake road.

Every curve in the road is familiar as I pass the old and worn-out homes. The old white two-story home with the wraparound porch is where the Midgett's live. The jasmine vines that artfully dangle from the porch rafters sprawl delicate yellow flowers in the spring, but are bare vines now. As a child, I would always hope Gran drove slowly past so I could get a glimpse of the overly short people who lived there. Not until I was well in my teens did I finally realize that the name "Midgett" would not be on their mailbox if it were only an adjective.

I have a dear familiarity for each family who live and had ever lived in the homes on the stretch of black tar back to town. Not personally of course, but through Gran. Gran knew everyone; where they were from; who their family was; what they did for a living; and what they did on their days off. I was grateful Gran did not live in my neighborhood as there would definitely be gossip to tell.

Driving Gran's blue Cadillac sedan, I literally floated down the road. Several people waved from their porches and mailboxes, looking surprised to see her car traveling to town. In actuality, their shock may have been due to the fact that the car wasn't swerving between lanes. The one restaurant within a thirty mile radius was packed with the same lineup of cars that are there for breakfast, lunch, and dinner. With the trees barren, I spot Gran's stately double porches as I drive up the dirt path lined with Southern magnolia trees. As I approach the homestead that was built in 1883, I can't help noticing that the crepe myrtle tree that shelters the north side of the house hovers well above the roof now. Its weathered trunk reminds me of Gran – old and strong. Even though I have a key, I decide to use the key stuffed under the umbrella stand on the front porch. I suddenly long to lift up the black spray painted urn to see the key that Gran last placed there.

I am not quite sure why I am surprised to find the house completely undisturbed, I study every picture frame, brass pig, and other trinket that has been in place for the last three decades. Nothing was out of position, not even now. I guess I was hoping one of two things. One, the house would be cleaned out and I wouldn't have to deal with the impending emotions; or two, the house would be completely intact and I would find Gran in her favorite rocking chair waiting for me to arrive.

I take a tour of the century-old home as if I have never visited, which satisfies a need to experience the home with fresh eyes. The two doors on the front porch make the home look like a duplex. However, the doors had served as two entrances when the home was both a doctor's office and a residence.

The primary door leads into the den which is shaped like a pentagon and accommodates a corner fireplace. This room is the most familiar to me because of hours spent gathered here with Gran. Gran displayed each of my class pictures from the ones with self-cut hair to the ones with horn-rimmed glasses. Every photo she received of Stella and Graham was squeezed amongst the multitudes of photo memories.

The formal living room, just off the main room, can be accessed directly by the other front door. However, anyone who knew Gran never used the opposing door. There was furniture placed conveniently in front of it to discourage the thought. Although the room was not off limits, it was rarely used over the years. Occasionally when I felt daring, I would sneak off and sit on the teal green chenille loveseat.

Just past the regal room is the adjoining dining area. My mind wanders picturing our many holiday dinners with a scrumptious menu, love, laughter, and prayers. It too, has a beautiful fireplace and mantle which houses gorgeous colored glass in shades of blue, pink, and gold. My favorite spot is a dry bar that was used for serving tea and water in antique teapots. It wasn't until recently that I opened its top to find that it had indeed held more than just tea. Bottles of liquor more than four decades old were hidden and obviously forgotten.

A dark hallway with floor-to-ceiling knotty pine paneling leads to a full bath and serves as a connector between the "old kitchen" and the original home. The bath is a narrow space with a tiny stand up shower, but it always felt large in functionality. Because it sits apart from the main living space, I relished the opportunity to take a shower in the cozy room with Gran's finest soaps and guest towels. An operable window in the shower made for an almost outdoorsy bathing experience. I would open it just enough to feel the breeze and smell the fresh cut of grass or the daffodils that were blooming underneath.

The "old kitchen" has an identifiable scent that will always be decipherable. With a mixture of smells sandwiched between Brunswick stew and ice box cookies, it seems as though Gran and Junie had just frozen their last batch of goodies. The final room on the first floor is the "new kitchen." It, too, has a fireplace that to my knowledge was never lit probably due to the fact that cooking kept that room warm. The small kitchen window above the sink is the perfect frame for the age-old crepe myrtle. Another project left undone, the window casing was cracked which allowed the scent of the crisp air to seep in. Perched prominently on the parquet counter is Gran's favorite appliance, a compact toaster oven. In a pinch, she would have undoubtedly cooked a turkey there if the need arose.

I wave to the fourteen year-old neighbor boy who is making the house look alive by blowing the last of the fallen leaves from the porch. This is a gesture from the community, not out of duty, but out of respect. Suddenly, I have an overwhelming sense of why Gran never wanted to leave her home.

~

The winding stairs to the second floor are absolutely unique; perfect for sliding from the top step to the bottom on a skinny or fat tailbone in about two seconds flat. I climb the steep steps to the top stoop and pause to wrap my hand around the top of the stairwell post, a large rounded finial the size of a bowling ball. Over the years, Gran had used the finial to steady herself before taking the unforgiving descent down the stairs. I can almost smell the Avon hand lotion as if she had just passed.

With no hallways upstairs, two additional fireplaces, three bedrooms, one bathroom, and a "room where we sit" are separated only by walls. Many a night was spent watching Jeopardy, Wheel of Fortune, and Lawrence Welk on the 25-inch black and white Magnavox. My favorite pastime was sneaking upstairs to catch a glimpse of the "stories" as Gran called them. To her, soap operas were not proper for a young girl to watch. I decided at an early age I wanted to get away from being proper.

My favorite room in the entire house is the "princess" bedroom which was also Gran's bedroom. As a child, it was strange to me that she and Papa had separate bedrooms; however, after having years of marriage under my belt, I finally understand this little saving grace. A prominent cherry dresser lines the powder blue wall and contains treasures from every one of Gran's passions. She loved all kinds of jewelry as long as it had flair. Two drawers are dedicated to the hundreds of pieces which are by no means considered fine, just every piece of costume jewelry imaginable. Gran never threw an add-a-bead or neckerchief pin away. I know every piece with my eyes closed just by its shape. These worthless items by monetary standards are priceless to me.

Prominent scuff marks visible on the dresser top are permanently etched in my memory. I vividly remember the clumsiness that caused them. Minutes before Papa's funeral I escaped the mass of people who hugged every nook and cranny of the house. Having snuck upstairs, I was anxious for a few moments alone to regroup before going to the church. Gran's makeup chair seemed like a perfect place for me to lay my head in my hands and quietly cry. At fourteen, I was sad for his death but was also confused and unsure of how to handle the loss.

While reaching for a tissue, I knocked over a cup of punch and within seconds, the pineapple ginger ale slush began to seep under the glass that protected the dresser top. There was no way I could lift the heavy glass but was too scared to ask for help from Gran or anyone else who was preparing for the funeral. Knowing this was neither the time nor place to have a crisis, I simply had to leave the chaos when Gran called my name to get ready for the funeral.

Later that evening while Gran removed her jewelry piece by piece, she looked down and saw the liquid saturation. I quietly recapped the unfortunate chain of events. After several minutes of listening to me try to recount the facts, Gran was as disappointed as I knew she'd be. Looking back, I knew her sadness of the furniture blemishes was the only thing she could control. She laid her head where mine had been just hours earlier and wept. That was the only time I ever saw Gran cry.

~

Lost in the remembrances of many years past, I was startled

by Scarlet's bark. As I make my way down the winding stairs to bear the cold for Scarlet's sake, Gran's bravery fills my heart and soul. The beams and columns that hold up the one-hundred year walls are no stronger than the fortitude and strength that kept Gran going for almost a century.

Chapter 4

Relieved to have some fresh air, Scarlet sniffs every possible nook and cranny of the yard. Thoughtful with my steps, I climb two unsteady cement blocks and slowly open two old doors to the smoke house. In recent years the dilapidated shack has served only as extra storage. As I reach for the light bulb cord, I hear rustling at the base of the dusty old floorboards. Knowing a creature is about to run up my legs at any moment, I tap open the door and jump clear over the cement block. The excitement catches Scarlet's attention as she trots in her fourteen year-old fashion to check things out. She puts her nose to the door and starts to wag her tail. If Scarlet, who is no hunting dog, smells something, it has to be big.

With my eyes shut tight, I stick out my arm as far as it could reach, but stand back an arm's length from the rickety door while slowly cracking it all the way open. There is an eerie silence with no signs of a snake, mouse or three-headed monster. I wait what feels like a lifetime and open the old door a little wider. All of a sudden a little gray head sticks out, too big to be a mouse or a rat. Still unsure of what's to come, I open it wider in time to see a tiny little kitten poking its body out of the crevice. Without thinking twice, I scooped the shivering kitten in my arms while I carefully looked in the nooks and crannies to make sure there were no more kitten surprises.

My questions and thoughts are interrupted as Charlie, the neighbor, turns off the leaf blower to check out the commotion. He tells me about a stray cat having a litter of kittens two weeks prior at another neighbor's house. After a bad storm he noticed the smokehouse door had blown open and thought the cat must have taken her kittens to the shed for shelter. The mother moved the kittens the next morning to a neighbor's porch and hasn't been seen since. Neighbors had taken the other three kittens under their care. The little guy in the shed must have gotten trapped, which was probably a good thing due to the cold.

After hearing the troubles the fluff ball has seen, I do not hesitate to wrap it in my sweatshirt and give it a new home. Scarlet, the kitten, and I make our way to warmth. Rustling through Gran's cupboards, I locate a perfect bowl to fill with water for the shivering kitten. As I stand in the same place Gran stood for more than seventy-five years, I see the crepe myrtle standing tall and strong. It's settled – the kitten's name must be Myrtle.

Scarlet is too old to be jealous or aggressive. As long as she gets to sleep and eat, life is good. Knowing the kitten has probably not eaten for several days, I take a leftover roll and soak it in water. Myrtle cannot get enough of the concoction. Feeling hungry myself but wanting to have a relaxed dinner at the lodge, the animals and I move upstairs to wrap up our efforts for the day.

~

The adjoining bedroom is separated only by walls, no hallways. Since the house was undoubtedly built from plans off a napkin, the floor plan seemed to be an afterthought. Even though the room is one door off the princess room, it was always treated as if it was a world away. The sacred room was Helen's old room. It was rarely used in recent years but felt heavy with presence. I imagined it just as if Helen had been there earlier that day. It did not seem as if anything had been moved out of place since the day she died. Going in the room always felt as if I was entering forbidden space and today seemed no different. There were no special knickknacks in a box or perfume that smelled like honeysuckle. There were only memories – ones that had been buried.

At the foot of the bed is a cedar chest filled with goodies. Every bingo prize Gran had ever won filled the seemingly endless box. From pink soaps that mimic shapes of animals to crocheted placemats, Gran collected a strange variety of keepsakes. As a young child, this particular chest was not off limits, but Gran had two cedar chests. One was filled with meaningless knickknacks and the other was filled with memories. As I move to open the second chest that has rested untouched for years, I realize I may be lost for hours.

The almost secret chest was not easily accessible like the other one. It was out of sight and out of mind. Handmade quilts with beautiful patterns and rich colors form a protective halo over the brown rectangular box. Careful in removing the century-old coverlets from the chest's top, I place them on the top shelf of the closet. With the chest almost staring at my soul, its significance is overpowering.

Deciding there is no time like the present, I carefully raise its top and am overcome by the smell of cedar. Overwhelmed by not knowing where to start, I struggle with digging straight to the bottom or starting at the top. I know when reading a book, I skip to the last page first which fits my Type A personality. However, for some reason, I feel as if today is different. I am going to slowly peel back the layers and not rush to the ending.

Folded in a perfect rectangle is a thin pale-green blanket. I carefully pick it up in my hands and hold it close to my cheek. I know this blanket of comfort – it was Gran's baby blanket. I am breathless as I realize that I am cradling a nearly century-old blanket that is perfectly intact. I lay it over my legs and tuck the ends under my toes. For a moment, I can feel Gran's wrinkled, but strong arms around me.

The chest's next layer is several inches deep filled with papers. Every wedding and funeral program Gran had ever received was saved in the trunk. Lying at the top of the pile is a wedding memento from Gran's high school neighbor, Macie. This wedding had the entire county talking. In a very small town, nothing gets past folks. Macie, a junior at the two-hundred student high school, was dating Chad, an outsider, from the Outer Banks. He was two years older than Macie and worked as a crabber in Avon. The two got hot fast, or at least "hot" for a small town.

The couple saw one another during the weekends and Chad occasionally picked Macie up from school. People started noticing and gossiping that she was getting thick around the middle. At first it was attributed to Macie's part-time job at the Dairy Queen; however, after a few months passed, only her stomach became larger. Despite the whispers and awkward glances, Macie and Chad kept their love intact.

One Sunday morning at church, Macie approached the altar during the last hymn of the service. As people began to notice her, their voices grew softer. The eighty-nine year-old organist, Mrs. Pearl, finally looked up at the altar and saw Macie kneeling down in front of the minister. With pure intrigue, she immediately stopped playing and stared along with everyone else in the pews. You could have heard a pin drop. All you could hear was the sound of whispering between the minister and Macie.

After a few minutes, Macie turned towards the people frozen in the pews and announced she was with child. With her voice shaking and a tear rolling down her freckled cheek, she declared that she would be marrying the love of her life, Chad. With her big blue eyes filled with tears, she pleaded to the congregation to allow them to marry in the church. People were stunned. No one moved, blinked an eye, or swallowed for what seemed like an eternity. Just as Macie was gathering her Bible to leave the church, the minister grabbed her hand, kissed it gently, and held it tightly for all to see.

The Reverend Stowe had shown his support in front of his congregation. Within moments, parents stood and started clapping. Row after row of people followed with their stand of support, too. Macie was overwhelmed with the support when she saw a glimpse of Chad who had been watching the whole scene from the balcony. He knew Macie was ready to tell their secret, but both had been scared about the repercussions. Her smile widened as she motioned for him to join her side. It was obvious to the small-town church that his heart was brimming with love and compassion for his pregnant Macie.

From ages two to ninety-two, people moved past typical expectations to unexpected blessings. Three months later, Macie and Chad had one of the largest weddings the church had ever seen. The pews were packed with the feeling of love pouring from the doors. Three weeks after their union, the newlyweds welcomed a baby girl into the community that has never let them down.

~

Next in the mound is Gran's corsage and program from my wedding. The two are wrapped daintily together with a wide silver satin ribbon. I carefully untie the bow and clutch the faded pale lavender rose corsage and can almost smell the roses and gardenias that banked the window sills, altar, and pews on our wedding day.

At the bottom of the pile of papers is a neatly folded newspaper clipping from Helen's death which looks as if it hasn't been touched in years. I carefully unfold each corner. Tucked in the middle of the newspaper is a dried yellow dandelion. As I begin reading the newspaper clipping, I realize that I rarely heard Gran speak of that day and certainly didn't know the details. As the details unfold, I learn Helen was hit by a car on the Lake Road. Gran and Helen were having a picnic on the June afternoon when a drunk driver hit and killed Helen on the spot.

I notice the time between the death and the funeral was right at a week. I remember an Aunt saying that Helen's body was kept at the house in the living room for family and community visitation for several days before the formal services. Apparently, back in the 40's, especially in the South, this practice was common place.

Below the epitaph was a poem written by Gran.

The time has come for you to leave this earthly place
You're entering the Kingdom and Heaven and seeing Jesus' face
The angels will hold you tight in their arms
You will never experience any more harm

For you were taken much before your time
We can't predict God's reason or rhyme
I will cherish the dandelion you picked for me
The image of you laughing is what I'll always see
Go now, be free, and know you are loved
For we will look for you in the clouds above
Love you forever.

Wiping tears from my cheek, I am overcome by the pain Gran must have felt and endured. I had never seen Gran vulnerable. This is the most insight I have ever had inside her world. The stoic, stern at times grandmother is finally humanized. She hadn't become strong with deep roots haphazardly; her trials and tribulations had given her that fortitude.

As I look out the window and see the day coming to a close, the night sky is settling in and casting a soft pink hue on the crepe myrtle. Wanting to see the last few moments of its beauty, I wrap Myrtle in the green baby blanket and lead Scarlet to navigate the winding stairs. As we make the steep descent, I unconsciously stall on each step and think about how it would have felt to walk in Gran's shoes. Would I ever feel as strong as Gran seemed?

Chapter 5

The blue sedan is almost on auto-pilot as it makes its way back to the lodge. Once there, Myrtle is hesitant with her new surroundings and closes in on my heels as I try to get out of my clothes. Knowing I'd need comfort clothes to go along with the comfort food, I had luckily packed yoga pants and Matt's old t-shirt. The ratty and tattered t-shirt will still be in my wardrobe when I'm old and feeble due to the fact that Matt was wearing this beat-up Duke t-shirt the first night we met. I was in Boston for my first bridal and formal wear buying trip for the shop at a ripe age of twenty-three. I decided to calm my nerves by doing some of the typical touristy sightseeing. It didn't take long to stumble upon the famed Bull and Finch Pub, aka Cheers. Not caring that I was alone, I decided to have a beer at the same spot Norm had placed his order time after time. The bar was surprisingly lively a few minutes after eight. After two beers and the purchase of a nostalgic Cheers sweatshirt, I was about to leave when I heard someone call my name.

"Sam, Samantha?"

The familiar voice was from David Bloom, co-counselor during my summer work at Duke's TIP program. Not believing my eyes, I ran over and threw my arms around his neck.

"How long has it been?" I asked David.

"Too long for sure. Sam, isn't this crazy we're reconnecting in Boston of all places?"

I felt a tap on my shoulder and saw someone holding a Cheers sweatshirt in the air.

"Is this yours? You dropped it when you hugged my buddy," said the stranger standing beside David.

"You know David? And, yes, thank you. This sweatshirt is my proverbial Boston tourist souvenir."

"Oh sorry, Matt this is Sam Harris. Sam, this is Matt London."

David motioned to the bar and threw a quick wave to a girl sitting there. She made her way through the crowd and joined David's side.

"Annie, this is Sam. She and I go way back when we would spend summers at Duke. She was the smart one," David said as he winked at me.

Annie and I exchanged greetings, and then quickly decided to get a table and have dinner. I instantly agreed as the two beers had made me a little light-headed since I had eaten little all day. I didn't want to look like a light-weight, or at least not yet.

Two hours quickly passed with talk of current work projects and details of past relationships. Annie and David met at Duke while both pursuing International Studies. Annie landed a job in Boston with a large company focused on foreign imports and exports. David stayed back to earn his MBA and used weekends to keep up their long distance relationship. I was not surprised that David and Annie were making a go of the relationship – he had always been very devoted to everything he put his heart into.

Matt and David met in the MBA program and became roommates. Matt had dropped out after one semester to pursue not what his parents wanted for him, but what he loved most – art. He quickly realized he could make money doing what he was good at and enjoyed. I found it fascinating that his family embraced his choices and didn't disown him for being different. Anything out of the course of great expectations wasn't allowed in my family. Matt's ability to think beyond what others wanted for him was definitely attractive to me.

A couple of drinks turned into four hours of laughter and anecdotes of times past. David laughed hysterically while recounting the story of us dancing the electric slide during the end of summer dance party. I had conveniently forgotten the fact that right in the middle of the stage, I fell off the front of the platform flat on my ass. Even though I had been head cheerleader in high school, grace was not my middle name.

As the night wound down and Annie left to take a call, I asked David how his dad was doing. Each July 4th I always think of David's family as the date marked the anniversary of his mother's death. It's a night that will be forever ingrained in my heart. Several of us were lying under the stars in the Duke Gardens watching the fireworks explode in the night sky when Brett, the Resident Advisor, came running up the hill shouting David's name. Barely able to speak from panting, Brett told David his dad had called and said he needed to get home right away as his mother had been killed in a Jet Ski accident on Kerr Lake.

Stunned with absolute shock and grief, David couldn't move. Every year the entire Bloom family celebrated the holiday at the lake.

David had been there for seventeen Fourths of July until this one. He had chosen to spend July 4th with his TIP friends as this was their last summer at Duke together before going off to college.

Knowing David shouldn't drive, I packed his clothes and insisted upon driving him to his family home in Henderson. We both knew my 1967 VW convertible might not make it down the road, but didn't dare speak of it. In fact, we barely spoke at all driving the monotonous path up I-85. There was no need for words. As we meandered down the dirt path of the winding road to the family home, I was amazed at the beauty of the surroundings. The home was a beautiful farmhouse situated perfectly on Kerr Lake. It looked like a Christmas tree with every room illuminated with the glow of lights and people. I helped David gather his suitcase and walked with him to the back porch. All I could see was the moonlight on the lake. It was as still and dark as night – vastly different than what was happening inside the home.

It was almost as if David knew it would be quiet behind the house. I could tell it was a familiar place of respite for him. He walked over to a dry-docked canoe, eased his lanky legs into the hull, sat down and laid his head in his hands and cried like a baby. Still saying nothing, I went over to the canoe, took a spot in front of him and put my head down on his. I could literally feel his pain. It was sharp and deep. He cried until he could cry no more.

We finally made it to the back steps and after pausing for what seemed like hours, we made our way into the emotionally heavy house. It was like a blanket of grief drenched us from head to toe. With dozens of people gathered around a table of food, David's dad insisted that I drink a cup of coffee before heading on the road again. Not wanting to cause a fuss, I graciously accepted the cup, using it to wash down coconut cake, pecan pie, and blueberry cobbler. I knew I wouldn't be hungry for days, but I dared not eat what was politely offered to me. Much later that evening, I left David and his family knowing that Fourth of July would never be the same. David came back to camp a week later and he wasn't quite the same either. I knew a part of his heart had died.

Now, with several years having passed, healing had obviously begun. David happily reported that his dad recently married his high school sweetheart. The memories with David, although painful, were important to reconnect us. We called it a night as David gave me a tight hug and I graciously shook Annie's hand. I offered my hand to Matt but to my surprise, he bent down and put his arms around my neck. His embrace was warm and kind. I reached up and grabbed the tops of his arms, accidentally feeling his biceps. His arms were strong and warm. I realized the embrace was a little long and quickly let go.

"I feel like he I've been with an old friend," Matt said with his ice blue eyes peering into my soul. Not wanting to seem too eager, I smiled and whispered, "Me, too."

As the group dismantled, we all vowed to get together once we were back in the Raleigh area, but I knew how these promises usually went. I didn't want to hold my breath, but secretly I was hoping.

By the time I got home to North Carolina, Matt had left several messages on my answering machine. We began to see each other and continued to click just as we did at the Bull and Bear. David remained a close friend as he and Matt continued to be roommates until Matt and I moved in together. After our wedding, David and Annie moved to San Diego for Annie's job. Other than Christmas card pictures and occasional Facebook updates, our communication has been sparse. However, we are forever indebted to David and Boston.

I think back to the wonder Matt and I felt for one another in those days. Wanting to learn about every inch of our being, we couldn't get enough of the tedious details. Now, we can hardly stay still enough for even a recap, let alone specifics.

~

My daze breaks with the sound of the cell phone ringing. With barely any service in the deep country, I rush to the window desperately trying to gain a few more bars. The ring tone, "Thriller," is merrily playing and I smile knowing Matt is on the other line. Graham, being the tech guru, downloaded the theme song and I can't for the life of me figure out how to change it. Now, it just makes me laugh. Eager to talk to the family, I quickly answer. Instantly, I hear two sweet little voices saying, "Hey, Mama." An even bigger smile covers my face as I realize Stella and Graham have called me on speaker phone.

With utter concentration, I listen to every detail of Graham's first Little League practice as he proudly recounts getting hit in the back with a ball. Stella played princess dress up with a new neighbor and had a tea party with grape Kool Aid. Wanting to break the news of our furry friend, I find a break in the conversation to tell them about Myrtle. Happiness ensues as I hear Stella yelling in the background that she is getting her blankies ready for the new kitten.

Graham insists that Myrtle will be sleeping with him. I hear the excited chatter as they fade away to get things prepared for Myrtle. Matt picks up the phone and instantly, I am calmed by his soothing voice. He obviously has things under control at the house. Learning to let go and allowing Matt to do things for the kids and their routines is difficult for me. The last couple of days have been easier for me to give up the details as responsibilities with Gran's house don't lend me much of a choice.

Matt pretends to be a captive audience listening to my day about finding items in the trunk, but he's obviously distracted by the kids' excitement. He finally realizes the root of their enthusiasm when Stella slows down long enough to tell him about the new kitty. To say the least, he is definitely a little surprised. I can't blame him too badly as I know he is remembering my strong allergy to cats. To soothe his apparent worry, I vow to use allergy medicine as soon as I return home. I also promise that at any sign of the slightest reaction to Myrtle while on medication, I will find her a new home.

Matt doesn't much believe in "signs from God" but I sure do. Wise enough not to rock the boat, I decide not to tell Matt that I believe I found Myrtle for a reason. Whatever it will take to disguise the least bit of allergic reaction, I will do it. I may be wearing sweats and turtlenecks in the summer, but if that's what it takes to keep my little gift from heaven, then that's what I will have to do.

We continue to talk a little more about our day. Without hesitancy, Matt says he will read the letters and memoirs I've unearthed. I know in my heart he will listen to each and every word when I get home. Matt has always been a listener and talker, but he is not good at either over the phone. Almost forgetting I have a business to run, I ask him to check on it the next day.

"Sam, please try and forget about the brides for a couple more days. Plus, half of them will be divorced within two years," he says with sarcasm.

I chuckle and realize this is the first time I've laughed in a couple of days and it feels good. On speaker phone, Matt, Stella, and Graham yell their love in unison, and I do the same back. This makes my day.

Realizing I haven't eaten all day, I peer at the multitude of sweets on the counter. Feeling tempted, I give them a thought but remember there's a package from Carrie sitting in the closet that sounds even better. As I open the coat closet door, reach to the top shelf for the Trader Joe's bag, I also see a hat box and I open that first. Pale yellow tulle is nestled among sheets of tissue paper protecting the delicate hat. As I peel back the tissue, a gorgeous pill box hat in the same buttercream that is used for the elegant veil is revealed. Without effort, I picture Gran dressed in one of her loveliest dresses with the hat perfectly perched on her head with not a hair out of place. She had such elegance and knew when and what to wear at every occasion. With my old t-shirt and yoga pants, I think the hat is a perfect addition to my ensemble. She would definitely look at me now and say, "Well, honey, you see all kinds."

Moving on to Carrie's surprise, I open the bag to find two bottles. Turning the first around, I see Boone's Farm Strawberry Hill and laugh out loud. The second bottle is my favorite Riesling label, Cupcake. Nestled between the two bottles is an envelope with a card and several photos.

The first photo is of me, Carrie, and Gran having a tea party in my old Holly Hobbie room. The caption on the back reads, "First Royal Tea Party – 1977." We were holding tiny little plastic teacups in our hands with our pinky fingers held high in the air.

The next picture is of me, Carrie, Gran, and Papa on Ocracoke Island. This caption reads, "My best vacation ever - 1982." I vividly remember taking the ferry to the island for a week's stay at Gran's brother's cottage. I chuckle, remembering Gran and Papa making us wear life jackets in the pool even though we were swimming in the kiddie end.

The third photo is unfamiliar. It captured Gran lifting the wedding veil over my face as she is wiping a tear from my cheek. The picture is priceless as it captured a rare moment in time. As I read the card from Carrie, I clutch the photos tightly and laugh out loud about the time we drank Strawberry Hill under the lodge's elm tree. The scene is clearly engraved in my memory. The night was hot and we were a ripe sixteen years old. Carrie had absconded with the bottle from her older boyfriend and packed it away for our weekend jaunt to the lodge. It was the best tasting drink we had ever had and we polished off the bottle. Too drunk to walk, we slept in a hammock under the limbs that protected us like a blanket.

Carrie's words flow from the card as if she was standing near. Tucked in the bottom of the bag is tissue paper wrapped around what feels to be a glass. As I carefully unwrap it, I instantly recognize the painted glass. Carrie and I spent a girls weekend in Boone for her thirtieth birthday and painted pottery and glassware at a local artist's studio. I had actually painted this glass for Carrie with her favorite inscription, "Live, Laugh, Love." I had no idea this wine glass still was in existence and am in awe of the thought of it making its way back to my hands.

Inside the glass is a curled up yellow piece of paper with a bow wrapped around it. I unroll it seeing Carrie's familiar calligraphy:

Your cup may seem empty for now

But fill it with your memories of someone dearly loved
Knowing that you are held close
Love you, mean it, always ~Carrie

Carrie has always known exactly what to do and say and when to do both. She has the kind of grace that is immeasurable. I decide not to waste the moment and without delay, I open the bottle of Boone's Farm trying not to think about its bitter taste. While I am remembering swigging from the bottle under the stars and the low branches of the elm tree with my best friend, I gag from what tastes like spoiled strawberries. I reluctantly put the sacred bottle of the teenage rite of passage in the trash and open what will definitely be easier to swallow, the bottle of predictable Riesling.

Settling by the fireplace with the glass of comfort, Myrtle in my lap, and Scarlet at my feet, I reach for the letters I'd found in the secret trunk and untie the pink satin ribbon. Roughly two dozen letters, some typed, others hand written, are awaiting my attention. The various papers are gorgeous. Some seem to be made of a thick tissue paper with others designed in dainty pastels with monogrammed initials. I recognize the monogrammed paper as my first piece of stationery purchased as a married woman. I chuckle as I realize that 15 years later, that same stationery box still is almost full. I used it with Gran because I knew it would please her. She always noticed the fine details of the paper and my black fine point ink pen. No one else in my world gives a rat's ass about the paper or even receiving a thank you note, but Gran sure did. A simple "thanks" in person or by phone has always been sufficient for everyone else. Nowadays, the preferred quick way to communicate is by texting or emailing. Almost ashamed to admit, I realize I am going to miss this ritual and formal way of communicating. From this day forward, I make a mental note to keep instilling the forgotten good manners to my own two children.

I read the note I sent to Gran aloud and watch as Scarlet and Myrtle's ears perk up as if they're listening.

My Dearest Gran,

Good morning! It is a beautiful spring day here in Raleigh and I hope you find the morning nice in Hyde, too. I got up early this morning because we got a puppy and she needed to go outside at 5:30am. We named her Scarlet because her fur has shades of red. She is not a mutt, she's a Heinz 57, a mix of the finest dogs around. Getting used to this puppy life sure is hard!

I wanted to tell you that we're certainly enjoying

your car. It's so comforting to know that we have a safe and reliable car to drive each morning. Matt drops me off at the store and then he heads a few blocks to his studio. If I need to run errands during the day to the bank, post office or getting lunch, everything is right down from the store. We really appreciate your thinking of us. Is your new Oldsmobile doing well still? Matt said he helped you figure out how to get the trunk open the other day when you called. When we see you next we'll help you figure out all the bells and whistles.

I am having a bridal gown expo in two weeks and would love it if you could come and join us. We'll be having a fashion show and hair and makeup makeover. If you could come and spend the weekend with us, we'd love it. You and I could make cucumber sandwiches, cheese straws and mints. If you'll bring your recipe for the ice cream punch, bowl and cups, I would appreciate it.

Call me if you can come and we'll be getting your room ready. Scarlet can't wait to meet you!

Love you,
Sam

The car Gran gave us was a 1987 Oldsmobile Ninety-Eight. It was dark red with a red leather roof. It was huge, almost boat like as a dozen people could have fit in the backseat. It replaced our VW Beetle and Datsun that were literally both on their last wheels. Gran had never had any car other than an Oldsmobile, which I associated as being an old person's car, but am forever thankful for my gray-haired car starting each morning without fail. Matt had never been about appearances, so he drove the "Love Boat," which he lovingly named, with pride.

I remember the weekend of the bridal expo well. It was my first open house and thankfully, Gran came to help. She didn't just show up and watch me run about crazily; she rolled up her sleeves, brought every good idea that was bound by an etiquette rule, and made the day perfect.

We made fine mints, beautiful finger sandwiches and served perfect punch for the event. Gran traveled with her recipe box filled with Hyde County's best recipes. She also supplied me with empty cards which I began to fill with recipes like cheddar cheese straws and sherbet punch. I still use the recipes with punch always making a big hit at wedding and baby showers. Graham and Stella will eat cheese straws almost any day of the week.

Sipping wine while reading letter after letter, I am thoroughly amused by the simple things that were written and realize life gets so complicated at times with noise. Just sitting down to drink a glass of tea and talking about the weather seems absolutely refreshing. The last time Matt and I slowed down just to talk about silly and inconsequential things was probably before the kids were born. The snippets of dialogue in the past few years have been solely centered on money, work, kids, discipline, with only occasional light-hearted banter.

Relishing in the quiet time alone, I fall asleep with a glass of wine in one hand and a letter I'd written Gran about falling in love with Matt in the other.

Chapter 6

Awakened by the sound of the grandfather clock tolling seven, Scarlet lifts her head and looks towards me in disgust as if she is wondering why I have woken her. Shivering from a slight chill, I smile and realize I am still wearing Matt's Duke shirt. Feeling close to him this morning and remembering why, I smile thinking about my night's dream about the two of us, much younger, traveling overseas. Part of the dream was true – we did travel to Europe but backpacked the economical way through the countryside while sleeping in hostels.

My level of fear is much keener now as I wouldn't dare go from town to town without knowing each detail of the trip before setting foot in a foreign country. Have I changed into a stodgy and uptight woman or is it possible that I have matured and am conscientious about keeping the family safe? In my twenties, thinking that I knew who I was, I am sure as sure can be that I didn't know then and still do not know now.

Needing to wake up quickly with the help of caffeine, I make a checklist of what I'd like to get done at Gran's house today while waiting for the first cup to brew. Today, organization is key so I can get back to Raleigh and keep life moving. Squeezing all I can in the trunk of Gran's sedan, I finish inside by freezing the remaining mounds of food from the funeral. Anxious to tell Matt about the letters Gran had saved, I phone him on the way to her house.

"Sam, please don't get overwhelmed so you stray from your task. You can read those letters when you get home," Matt says in an annoyed tone.

I quickly dismiss him by saying, "I will take care of everything, just as I always do."

I worked hard, allowing myself to stop, breathe, and get lost in the moment with the letters. How could he be lecturing me on what should be happening with my time? Realizing the quiet place in my heart and soul is healing, I suddenly become frightened that it will be lost upon returning home. The drive through the quiet countryside is savored as I listen to absolutely nothing but my heartbeat and Gran's spirit.

"Well, Scarlet and Myrtle, I guess we MUST stay on task today," I say to my adoring furry friends as I unlock what feels like an empty home.

I start out by focusing on papers that seem important. In awe of the multiple financial commitments Gran successfully managed before and after Papa's death, I smile, picturing her talking business to any man within a hundred miles. People always called her stubborn, but Gran corrected them by saying she was independent. Well aware people say the same about me, I am now proud of the term that used to be irritating.

The last box of photo albums and memoirs is loaded in the car. Not quite ready to leave, I make the upstairs trek one more time. My heart truly aches as I reminisce about memories I've had in the house for more than three and a half decades.

"If these walls could talk," I mutter passing my hand along the old walls.

The stately house that was once warm with people and pone bread now sits stoic and silent.

~

The creaky door to the second level porch reveals a worn out floor. From wear and tear, the handrails and spindles are barely attached. Taking a seat in the middle of the floor, I picture my baby dolls situated on the rustic gray floor having a tea party. I would spy people coming down the street and slide in close to the wall as if they couldn't see me hiding in the open air porch. This was my hiding place and secret little world.

With one last big task ahead, I decide it's time to address the inevitable – Gran's will. Hurriedly reading through the legal jargon, I pause to realize Gran would not be proud of my imprudence. The words are predictable until the last paragraph which requests a handful of wildflower seeds be planted under the old elm tree at the lodge. The only caveat is the timing of June third, which was the day Helen died. It all comes clear as I picture the colorful blanket of flowers covering the base of the tree. Finally, after all these years, I can appreciate why the beautiful flowers are so prolific under the elm tree.

My mind flashes forward to June when the kids are typically knee deep in school and sports. Will I remember to do this important task? Knowing failure is not an option, my thoughts quickly turn to making Gran's wish happen. In her perfect fashion, Gran left specific notes on the exact place to plant the flowers along with a note in an envelope. Surely she didn't expect this note to remain unopened. Having self-control to leave this letter untouched until June will be the real challenge. Leave it to Gran to tie up loose ends until the day she died.

~

The nearly four hour drive back to Raleigh extends my reflection time until my phone starts ringing nonstop. First, Graham yells news of winning Student Government Association Treasurer. While talking a mile a minute about the win, he quickly pauses to ask what a treasurer actually does. My long-winded explanation must have bored Graham because he quickly said, "See you soon" and hung up.

The second call is Carrie announcing she has secured an appointment for the Governor's daughter and wife to look at gowns two days later. She is as kid-like as Graham with her excitement. With her filling in the past few days at *je t'aime*, my worries have been non-existent. Little does she know that my secret hope is for her to leave the outside sales world to become part owner of the boutique.

The third call is Stella saying she has prepared a nest of sorts for Myrtle. Apparently, her doll blankets and pillow are bundled in a box for Myrtle. Without a doubt, Stella has every intention that this little kitty will be her newest doll.

With the iPod cranked, I wail tunes of my second love, Dave Matthews. Myrtle climbs behind my neck and sleeps at the top of my shoulders the entire trip home. So glad to be thrust into normalcy, I am not even phased by Raleigh rush hour traffic.

~

As I pull into the driveway, Graham is practicing his golf swing in the front yard while Stella is painting Myrtle's new kitty box. I bite my lip as Graham swings his chip shot into the new shoots of fescue grass and sends the tender green blades flying. I keep reminding myself of what is important.

Stella and Graham come running to give hugs as they quickly fly past me to open the doors to search for Myrtle. Her steel gray fur blends in with the upholstery which keeps her camouflaged for a few moments. The first to spy Myrtle, Graham carefully picks her up and tucks her into his arm. After half a second, Stella demands her turn and after being passed back and forth, Myrtle gets so exhausted she falls asleep in mid air.

I open the front door to the comforting smell of spaghetti sauce that's been simmering all day. Matt comes out of his workroom obviously startled by my presence.

"I can't believe you made it home early. I thought you'd be curled up on the sofa reading decades of stories about the pig prices of 1958."

Matt makes up for his joke by scooping me up and planting a great big kiss on my neck as I finish tasting the simmering sauce. Matt nibbles the evidence from my bottom lip. Excited about the dinner and not wanting to disappoint, he completes the final preparations.

Dinnertime is spent catching up on the past few days. The kids eat in record time in order to play with Scarlet and Myrtle. Scarlet nips at Myrtle as if she's claiming her stake with the kids, but that lasts only two seconds because Graham gives Scarlet his dinner scraps.

"Moooooom, I want Myrtle to sleep with me," Stella somehow manages to make my name five syllables.

Graham quickly retorts. "But Mom, that's not fair."

"Sweeties, you two have to figure it out. She is our new family pet and I want you guys to figure this out together."

For the next few minutes Matt and I overhear the kids fussing over who is sleeping with her until a pivotal moment happens - they decide to have a sleepover in the family room so Myrtle can be with both of them. And happiness ensues.

It is very easy to see that Matt has done a hell of a job keeping the kids and the house intact. I am not absent very often which doesn't give them much practice, but I am most relieved and pleasantly surprised. After the kids and animals are settled I slip on nothing but a red thong and lock our bedroom door. Matt puts down his mystery novel, takes off his glasses, and does a double-take. His graying blond hair is distinguished looking and I think he looks sexier than he ever has.

I make love to him out of deep appreciation and gratitude for the love we share and the family we've built. I fall into a deep sleep on top of him feeling like I'm truly at home again.

Much to my dismay, the clock goes off early the next morning. Remembering our night before, Matt hops on top of me hoping to have a morning delight until we hear tapping on our door. We make a date to finish this later and open the door to find Stella holding her Halloween candy bucket with Myrtle peeking out. Matt and I both couldn't help but smile at the sight.

Chapter 7

Reality calls like a cold shower which forces me to take a moment to breathe slowly and deeply. This is the first day back in normal life, or as normal as life can be at any point. Peace in my world, after the fastest twenty-four minute race around town you have ever witnessed, ensues after the first click to unlock the door of my wedding boutique, *je t'aime*. The therapeutic ritual of placing the bountiful pots of seasonal annuals beside the wrought iron bench sets me in the mood to encounter anxious brides, jealous bridesmaids and neurotic mothers. If the bench, placed perfectly centered in front of the bay window, could write a book, it would be the best selling combination of mystery, romance, and parenting how-to books ever printed.

With the kids at school, lunches packed, and the dog walked, I can begin to focus on coping with my daily routine again. I can't pick up the phone for advice and comfort from Gran. I'll have to draw on the peace and strength from within. Seeing the cheerful pink and white striped awning of *je t'aime* gives me the courage to start my day.

Glad I mustered the courage to get back into my routine, I instantly spot an enormous bouquet of peonies, eucalyptus, and gardenias sitting on the entrance table of *je t'aime*. Around the base are rose petals scattered in pastel colors. A card is tilted against the base which reads "Samantha Lynne." Only four people in the world still call me that and one of them just died. I open it and instantly recognize Matt's artistry on the front of the card.

Just about the time I wipe away a tear, Carrie unlocks the front door with her perfect timing. Wiping a tear from my cheek, she says, "By the way, if Matt has a clone, I want him."

She instantly lightens the mood by telling me the details of *je t'aime* in my absence.

As Carrie finishes a couple of orders to show me, I slip away to call Matt.

"You know I must have really wanted to make love last night because I didn't even know about the flowers." I say coyly. "Seriously, you'll never know how much the flowers meant to me today."

We chat for a couple of moments but before hanging up, Matt says, "By the way, you owe me."

~

Carrie gives great details for the three wedding party orders she took along with the potential order for the Governor's family.

"I will fill in for you anytime." Carrie says earnestly. Halfway into her car I hear her yell, "By the way, I am coming back on Saturday to help with the celebrities!"

I am used to people making appointments and not showing up, but Carrie feels confident the Governor's family means business. No matter the result, I am energized by Carrie's excitement.

Using the quiet time of the morning, I order the Matheson's wedding party dresses. The bride has chosen a white strapless shantung silk gown with intricate brocade details on the bodice and train. The attendants are wearing knee-length strapless taffeta butter-yellow dresses which seems odd to me as the wedding is a high noon affair. I remember the bride from earlier dress browsing and recall her telling her bridesmaids that they will not be wearing the long dresses that her mother wanted them to wear if it was over her dead body. Often, I will step in and try to coax families to agree, but I knew to stay away from this beehive. The good news is that the bride's mother signed the order so there should be no surprises.

The second order is from a bride that I had the pleasure of helping with her first and second weddings. Charlotte Hunter had given me business twice before and thank goodness did not blame her wedding gown for the demise of her previous two marriages. She ordered a strapless little number this time in white. I chuckle out loud as I think about what Gran would say about this bride wearing white.

Charlotte's attendants are different from wedding to wedding, and somehow she's ended up with a large wedding party of eight. With this wedding, they will wear dresses with a crinoline. I don't even have samples that match this description. I see notes from Carrie that they're having a Southern Belle themed wedding and added a little smiley face beside it. Good grief, Carrie must have worked hard to search for the Scarlet O'Hara gowns. At least Charlotte has the guts to retry marriage so why not shake it up this time?

The last order is a new bride, Anna Noble, whose name is unfamiliar. Carrie did not finish the groom's last name so I can't quite complete the order. However, the groom's name, Andy L., sounds familiar as I type his partial name and Greenville address into the computer. I'm sure there are a thousand Andy's in Greenville. Even though I can place an Andy L. from Greenville at one time, I am sure there is no correlation because the Andy I knew would be nearly forty and probably married with a house full of kids.

Anna has exquisite taste as she chose a raw silk ivory simple gown with spaghetti straps and delicate crystals scattered from the waist down to the floor length gown. The attendant party will be wearing black silk with the similar bodice look but knee length which is appropriate for their five o'clock outdoor wedding. A note attached from Carrie says the groom will be stopping in to choose tuxedos within the next week. I decide to wait and complete the order when he shows.

~

The quiet day is a nice continuation of my time alone. I get caught up on work odds and ends and ease back into it all. Ready to get home, I wrap up what I could and head straight to my family.

Stella, Graham, and I settle back in to our daily routine. They seem almost as glad as I am to have routine back. Even though Matt kept them going, they waivered from their normal schedules and Graham, especially, likes and needs routine. Matt, with his artistic nature, goes with the flow much more easily.

A ritual in the house is to eat dinner together as much as possible. This nightly tradition started for me as a child when Gran would always bring the day to a close with dinner and conversation. The food wasn't the big deal as we would sometimes eat biscuits with a tomato and other times a rump roast. But what was important was the time to gather and connect after a long day.

As I formed my own family Gran would routinely call right after the dinner hour and check in. I think that was her way of having the same time together over the phone. Tonight there is extra chatter at the table as we take turns naming one good, one not-so-good, and one funny thing that happened to each of us throughout the course of the day.

Stella leads us off by announcing, "My good thing that happened was I was chosen to be the line leader. My bad thing is that my teacher, Mrs. Franklin, thinks our classroom hamster, Fluffy, only has one eye."

"Stella, you're making that up!" Graham teases her as he snickers at her statement.

"I am not. If you don't believe me, come by tomorrow after school and I'll show you how Fluffy won't open one of her eyes and we know it's not there because Justin saw it pop out." Stella says emphatically.

Graham begins to interrupt her again but she finally blurts out, "My funny thing is that when I came home I couldn't find Myrtle and found her sleeping way under my covers on my bed!"

Graham, being a typical fourth grader, often chooses to limit his dialogue and tonight was no exception.

"My good thing was that I got to play soccer at recess. My bad thing was forgetting my homework this morning."

Matt pipes up reminding him that he ran it to him during first period.

"Oh yeah, thanks Dad," he says before moving on to his funny moment of "watching Stella trip on the concrete walk after school."

While Graham's jab is not very nice, I realize Stella has as little grace as I do. My strong suit is not walking with steadiness and, unfortunately, Stella has taken after me. The good news is that Stella's strength is dance, especially modern and any type of creative movement. She is a soul who thrives on doing her own thing and dancing gives Stella the outlet she needs.

"Kiddos, I am leaving for an art show tomorrow morning and will be gone a few days. Will you help me pack after dinner?"

"I'll help you, daddy. You can even take my blankie if you want. Where are you going?" Stella's sweetness is as genuine as apple pie.

"Stella, I would love to take your blankie, if you're sure you won't miss it. This year the show is in Chicago." Matt says in a comforting tone.

"I forgot your show is here already. Has it been an entire year already? With the funeral and all that has been going on, it completely slipped my mind. Are you ready? Is your art done?"

"You've had a little bit on your mind. I've actually been finishing things up during the evening hours while you were in Fairfield. I really think I have a great portfolio this time."

"I am sure you do. Anyone you know going this year?"

"I've actually had a couple of people email me to say they want to have lunch. Not sure what that's all about, but I'll go for conversation and a free meal."

Matt begins a march to the bedroom with Graham and Stella eagerly following. Graham takes the lead and directs the brigade with Stella jumping on her dad's back.

Later in the evening after packing lunches, cleaning up the kitchen and paying bills, I pick up the phone and dial Gran's number to check in. For the first time in more than 35 years, I realize I can't call my treasured grandmother anymore. My heart sinks a little deeper tonight as the realization of loss sets in hard.

Feeling a little emotionally drained, I am hoping Matt won't cash in on my morning promise. Much to my relief, he is snoring his way into a deep sleep. I carefully pull his covers up, turn off the light, and tip-toe to my side of the bed.

Just as I am about to drift off to sleep, my thoughts turn to the name Andy. The Greenville connection is definitely a far-fetched coincidence, but it is still nice to remember him as I enter my night dreams.

Chapter 8

The next morning I keep myself busy in the boutique rearranging displays and unpacking shipments. It always makes me a little nervous when Matt travels alone. Until I get the "I'm safe" call, I plan to keep myself occupied.

I step away momentarily to the storage room to gather a new jewelry display when I hear the front door bells chime. Heading back to the front, I yell "Be there in a sec." In my clumsy fashion, I balance the awkward display and notice a man looking at a rack of wedding gowns.

"Hi, may I help you?"

The tall dark haired gentleman turns towards me with his hands held out. "Please, let me help you with that."

"Thanks, I guess I do have my hands pretty full."

I move the flower arrangement from Matt to the front register counter and pat the center of the table as a motion for the man to set the arrangement in that spot.

After a quick repositioning of the display, I turn around and extend my hand to the stranger. "Thank you for your help and how may I help you today?"

The gentleman removes his Nike hat and extends his hand to mine. I notice his boyishly tousled hair before he puts his hat on backwards.

"Haven't we done this before?"

Taken aback, I stutter, "I, I, I don't know what you mean," dropping my hand.

Who is this guy? Normally people don't come to a bridal shop to pick up women.

Oddly, the fellow chuckles and turns his hat back around. As he does, I immediately notice the East Carolina University college ring. Instantly, my knees go weak. As I catch my balance on the table, I slowly steady the jelly in my legs.

With my cheeks three shades of red, I finally babble, "It can't be you…Andy? Andy from Greenville?"

"I do believe it's me which makes you, Sam, Samantha Lynne from Greenville." (Oh yeah - one of the four people in the world who calls me that.)

Without pause, I throw my arms around his neck not believing it is really him.

"This is a lot different from the rudeness you showed me the first time we met in the print shop."

I reach up to hit the top of his hat and we both laugh.

"Why are you here? Where do you live now?" I ask as I begin to tabulate hundreds of questions in my mind.

"My fiancée, Anna, told me to come here and pick out my tux since I guess we're getting married in a few months. Sam, I'm pretty damn impressed with your place."

As it comes clear now that Andy is the "mystery groom," I regroup as if I'd never pondered his name the past few hours.

"Oh, yeah, this old place. I love what I do. Do you live in Raleigh, too?" trying to quickly turn the conversation back to him.

"No, not yet. I'm still in Greenville for the time being teaching at ECU. Teaching is still my thing and harassing print shop workers is still my gig, too."

"Oh, I'm sure." God, he has not changed one bit since I last saw him fifteen years ago.

"I hate to take up your time since you look really busy moving around displays and all, but I would really enjoy coming back around noon to catch up over a cup of coffee."

"Alrighty then - you don't have to twist my arm. There's a great coffee shop on the other side of Cameron Village if you'd like to pick two cups up on your way back."

"Great, still a coffee snob?" Andy asks as if he already knows the answer.

"You better believe it."

"See you in a bit."

I hurry to the corner window to watch him walking down the sidewalk. He takes off his hat again to rub his hand through his thick dark hair and subtly shakes his head. He seems a little shaken, too.

~

Lost in a daze, I wonder if I have seen a ghost. How, with all of the bridal stores in North Carolina, did Andy end up at mine and without his fiancée? Where do we pick up after all the lost time? My mind races back to the early nineties and I feel overwhelmed as my heart and mind are flooded with memories.

A month before the first day of my long-awaited senior year, Gran, wanting me to have a different high school academic and social life outside of Hyde County, sent me to live with a Methodist music minister and his family in Greenville. In exchange for room and board, I helped instruct the youth choir. For extra money during my senior year of high school, I worked at East Carolina University's print shop on the weekends, which is where it all began. Running print jobs for professors and staff during off hours was a perfectly mindless job which was a relief during a grueling academic year.

My first encounter with Andy began one Saturday night just minutes before midnight. Hearing nothing for hours except the copier, I was startled when the door opened, but calmed after realizing the store was accessible only by key. A young, preppy, and scholarly looking fella sauntered in wearing Duck Heads and a plaid button-down polo with the shirttail hanging out.

The handsome but amazingly annoying guy seemed surprised and almost put off that I was there. He barked, "Where's Ben?"

Startled by both his good looks and abruptness, I was quick to respond. "He works on the weekday shift now and I'm closing up here in fifteen minutes. Is Ben your buddy and that's how you got a key? The good old boys club?"

There, back at you, I thought.

"Actually, I am a TA for Dr. McBride in the Philosophy department and I don't appreciate your assuming I shouldn't be here."

I nodded as if I knew what TA meant, but actually had no earthly idea. "Oh, sorry, well, why are you here?"

"I was checking to see if Ben wanted to have a drink, but I also have a job going for Dr. McBride that I turned in yesterday."

Wanting to prove him wrong, I glided over to the job folder and searched the list for Dr. McBride. Damn, sure enough, there it was.

"Oh, okay, well sorry your friend isn't here and sorry your job isn't ready."

Andy flipped his hand as if to say "what a waste of time" and left.

The next weekend about the same time, Andy reappeared at the print shop door. Eyeing him in the reflection of the glass, I waited for him to say something. After a moment, he cleared his throat while I faked surprise at his presence and made my way to the desk.

"Oh, hello. Can I help you? Ben's not here. You can find him here on Monday."

Andy reached out his hand looking like he was starting fresh.

"Hi, my name is Andy Latimer and I'm a Teacher's Assistant

for Dr. McBride. We started out on a lousy foot last Saturday and I wanted to try this again."

Relieved to finally understand the meaning of TA, I relaxed a little, shook his hand and returned the gesture.

"Hi, my name is Samantha, Sam for short, and I am not a TA or college student. I am a senior at Rose High School. I work here on the weekends as you already know."

We continued shaking hands for several seconds when we both realized we hadn't let our hold go and quickly dropped the hand grip.

"Nice to meet you, Sam, and I'm sorry for the way I acted last Saturday. I am hoping to make it up to you. How about a drink?"

My face turned beet red. "Uh, uh, I can't yet. I mean, I'm not old enough. Plus, I need to close up here and be home by midnight."

"I'm so sorry, you just told me you were a senior, but you look older and sometimes I say things without thinking. I'm an ass." Andy was obviously backpedaling from his embarrassment.

"How about I help you close up and walk you out?"

Gran had a golden rule about not talking to strangers and I felt myself breaking this rule faster than my mind could stop me. Oddly, he didn't even feel like a stranger the weekend before when we had our rough start. I handed him two boxes with Dr. McBride's print job.

"Sam, I actually don't care about the print job. It's not why I came. Since you're trying to diligently do your job, I'm telling you now that I will come straight here Monday morning and pick up the job," Andy teased.

Realizing he was desperately trying to make amends for our first meeting, I quickly tidied up my jobs and left a couple of notes for Ben. We walked slowly down the stairs to the front of the building. Even late at night, the campus was buzzing with activity which always made me feel safe leaving, but the butterflies in my stomach made me realize I was glad I wasn't alone.

We chatted about his major, Philosophy, and my plans for college. After about an hour of talking, I looked at my watch and realized I needed to respect my curfew.

"Andy, I hate to cut this short, but I do need to get home."

"Are you sure? Stay just for a few more minutes?"

Knowing I had already pushed the envelope with leaving work early, I knew I needed to get home. In case I never saw him again, I didn't want to prolong our evening because it was starting to feel too nice.

"Um, I'm sorry. I really want to but it's getting late."

"Well, I am the one losing out. Samantha, I am just glad to have had some time to chat. Did I redeem myself?" His charm was overflowing from every orifice in his body at this point.

"Hmmm, maybe a little." I added playfully.

"Well then, that must mean that I have more work to do. How about we do this again on Sunday night for dinner?"

I much too quickly replied yes and began counting down the hours until our next meeting.

Chapter 9

I ditched playing piano for the children's choir practice at church on Sunday in order to meet Andy for dinner. Even worse is the white lie I told to the music minister about having a group project that could only meet Sunday night. Because of his gracious nature, he didn't think twice about letting me go which laid on the guilt as heavy as our summer humidity.

Sitting in traffic made the drive almost intolerable as I had time to be knee-deep in my guilt about lying to a holy man. However, the feeling subsided pretty quickly when I saw Andy standing at the front door of Darryl's Restaurant talking to a couple of guys. His madras shorts, polo crew shirt, and perfectly messy hair with the five o'clock shadow on his face made me say a quick thank you prayer.

Like a gentleman, Andy introduced me to his friends. Although glad that Andy didn't mind me meeting his fraternity brothers, I was even more relieved when he led the two of us to our table. We had the night to ourselves and food seemed irrelevant as we talked incessantly for hours. Feeling childish about having a curfew, I decided to show Andy I was all grown-up by ending the night with an embrace that was meant to shoot chills up his spine. It was the kind of body-to-body connection that was almost electric. I was ready to lock lips hard, but still a gentleman, Andy landed a tender kiss on my lips. I knew that from this day forward, the menial hourly print shop job would go down in history as the most important job I would ever have.

~

The following Saturday night was spent bustling around so I could leave the print shop early. Andy showed up promptly at nine, allowing us to leave twenty-three and a half minutes later. Feeling giddy but not wanting to come across as immature, I couldn't resist the temptation to throw my arms around his neck and continue our last kiss. So, without refrain, I did just that in the middle of the college print shop complete with the smell of chemicals and ink. With doors locked and no one around, we had our first real kiss.

Weeks of much of the same ensued as we learned about one another in a way I never thought was possible. It was the deepest emotional connection that I felt sure either of us had ever encountered. My attraction to him increased each moment and I knew we were building more than a trite relationship.

Andy became a regular in the print shop on Saturday nights. My skills quickly sharpened and I became an expert at running around like a chicken with my head cut off so I could get done in half the time. After months of the same, we were not quite ready to call it an evening and walked to Elm Street Park. We talked about everything under the sun for hours, extending past my curfew. Having made the landing at the top of the slide our home for the evening, neither of us were ready to say our goodbyes.

Andy unzipped his jacket and laid it on the wood planks. He gently leaned me back and began kissing me with his gentle ways, but within minutes we were smoldering. The passion was overwhelming. As he began unbuttoning my shirt, I felt a rush of passion and anticipation that was and still is indescribable. Andy wanted me and I sure as hell wanted him. After several minutes of heavy breathing, he put my shirt back on, taking care to button each hole. This act alone almost sent me pouncing back on top of him. Knowing he had to be the strong one, he took my hand and walked me back to the car.

Barely able to talk from breathing so hard, I was sure he undoubtedly knew my passion and desire. We didn't need to say a word except for making plans to see one another the next day. We both knew we had to drive away or we would never be able to leave.

~

After lying to the church minister once, I decided I could not continue to ditch my church commitment the next evening, so we agreed to meet at Andy's dorm room right after I was finished with choir rehearsals.

My arrival at Aycock Dorm was precisely at six thirty. Luckily, someone was walking out and held the door so I didn't have to buzz Andy's room. Calculating my every step, I walked slowly to his room, not because I didn't want to get there, but because I was afraid I was on the verge of running.

The door was cracked, but still decided to knock. There was no answer but I clearly heard Eric Clapton cranked loudly so I decided to slowly nudge the door open. "Wonderful Tonight" was the ideal musical backdrop against Andy's perfect silhouette as he crouched over the sink to shave. His strong arms and lean torso glistened as water from his jaw line dripped down his chiseled body. Wearing only jeans with his boxers peeking out, I stared at the picture of sexiness for longer than I knew I should.

Finally, Andy saw me in the mirror and with shaving cream still forming a white beard on his face, he took me in his arms as if he hadn't seen me in days.

"Sorry I'm not quite ready. I just played football with the guys and got a quick shower. I was running a few minutes late."

"I'm sorry I got here early, but I'm glad I did," I said rubbing shaving cream onto his chest.

"Where is your roomie?"

"He won't be back until tomorrow. His first class isn't until noon and he won't dare come back a minute before. Plus, I paid him twenty bucks not to," Andy said between kisses on my neck.

Both secretly knowing it was a façade, we placed our books on the twin mattress and pretended as if we were there to work. Andy began to lecture me on how important the senior year is and not giving up during my last semester. After the first couple of sentences I stopped hearing him and focused on his beautiful blue eyes. I knew, without a doubt, then and there, he had changed me forever.

Sensing my intensity, Andy immediately assumed something was wrong.

"Sam, are you uncomfortable here? Here alone? We can go to the library to study if you'd like."

Knowing words couldn't begin to describe my comfort with him and our time alone, I decided to show him how I felt. Barely breathing, I took the lead by kissing his forehead down to his toes.

"Sam, please don't stop, but I need to do one thing." Andy jumped up to close and lock his door. It was obvious that he wanted complete privacy. He also restarted "Wonderful Tonight" and pressed the repeat button on the boom box. I smiled as I realized we were both thinking the same thing. While he closed the blinds, I slipped off my tank top leaving only my denim mini skirt and bra.

This time there was no holding back. We had gotten to the same point as the night before but this time I could tell neither of us wanted to stop. Andy began to unzip his jeans, but I stopped his hand as I wanted to do the honor. I knew what I was getting myself into and it felt right.

He gently pulled down my silk underwear and said he had "taken care of everything." I knew exactly what he meant and I let myself go. The night was all ours. Nothing else mattered. Wanting the intense connection to never fade, we made love twice. Andy treated me with the tenderness I had always dreamed of, but also made me feel like a woman. His body pressing against mine created the safest world possible.

In just hours, I had matured years. I had totally forgotten the original plan of our study session as we never once thought about food or cracked open a book.

~

The days mirrored that Sunday afternoon for months. Andy became part of my daily life, bringing me lunch at school and waiting for me at cheerleading practice. Not worried about my age and place in life, he and his friends would come to games to see me cheer. At least once a month I would skip a class that I was acing and slip into the back of a classroom where he was teaching. It felt as though I was the only person in the auditorium watching the most intelligent, sexy, handsome and charismatic TA that had ever existed at any university.

The passion and dream of our future together started to fade when Andy was given the opportunity to study abroad at Oxford the next fall. I had accepted a scholarship to UNC Chapel Hill and would also be leaving Greenville. Foolishly, we initially had no doubts about the strength of our relationship. We tried calling, but the inter-continental time difference was too hard to manage with the lack of mobile phone and texting capabilities that are commonplace today. To this day, my heart sinks when I contemplate the notion that the technologically savvy world we live in today would have saved us.

During Christmas break of our first semester apart, I jumped at an incredible opportunity to visit Hawaii with Carrie's family and didn't dream of declining the invitation. Unbeknownst to me, Andy was coming home for the holidays and we missed each other by twenty-four hours. Time passed and our talking faded, too, so I buried the chapters of our time together.

Chapter 10

Reality hits and forces me to snap out of the reminiscent daydream as I recognize Matt's ringtone and realize his flight landed safely.

"Hey, Sam. I just touched down," Matt says cheerfully.

"How was the flight?"

"It was fine once I had a bourbon and coke. You know I don't like flying without you. Oh, my cab is here."

"Have a successful and good time, babe. I pray your artwork makes the trip okay. Call me later."

"I hope it does, too. I'll find out once I check in. I'll talk to you guys later. Love you, Sam."

"Love you, too, Matt."

Good thing Matt's call derailed me from continuing down memory lane.

My phone rings again, playing Fergie's "Glamorous," the ring tone reserved for Carrie.

"Hey sweetie! What's up?" I ask cheerily hoping to disguise my anxious feelings.

"Oh you know – just a healthy dose of a shitty morning. My biggest client decided they would pull their advertising. Can you believe that? Are you still ready for me to be a business partner still?"

"You and I can run this store together at any moment. Your worst day would not have one-tenth the kind of stress you deal with on a daily basis now."

"Another morning like today and we're opening a bottle of champagne and signing a business deal. Actually, the real reason I called is to see if you have lunch plans. I'm going to be seeing a client at Cameron Village and thought I'd stop by."

Looking at the clock, I realize the morning is fading quickly. It is already half past eleven, an hour since Andy left the store. Have I been lost in time for that long?

"Oh yeah, lunch. I forgot it's about that time. Actually, I need to hang around here and get some things done." I say hesitantly as I know she's had a rough morning.

"Well, I can bring lunch to you there and we can eat at the store. I want to make sure you're eating and taking care of yourself. I know what happens to you during stress and it's my job to make sure you're letting me in to help you with your grief." Here goes Carrie's motherly tone again. Little does she know my mind is racing not due to grief but seeing Andy again.

"Thank you, sweetie. I truly do appreciate that you care, though it's been good for me to get back into the swing of things. Maybe we can catch up tomorrow?"

Sensing my insecurity, Carrie prods.

"Sam, what's going on? Is there something we need to talk about?"

"Damn, I can't keep anything from you..."

"Nor should you, my dear."

"The reason lunch is not good is because I actually have an appointment during lunch."

"Okay, go on..."

"You remember the order from Anna, the bride whose fiancé was coming back?"

"Of course..."

"Well, he came back, today."

"Oh, that's great! I hated taking a pending order and I'm glad to know the bride was on the up and up," Carrie announces almost proud of herself.

"Oh, he came all right. Carrie, you'll never believe who it is." The silence felt like hours.

"Samantha Lynne, tell me. Tell me!"

"Do you remember Andy from Greenville?"

"What, remember Andy? You're kidding me, right? Of course I remember. Wait, he's the mystery fiancé?" she asks trying to catch up.

"Yes to all of those," I whisper almost as if reality just hit.

"The bride was young, in her mid twenties. I wonder if this is his second marriage. What's the deal?"

Carrie says in a light-hearted tone. She has no clue where my heart has been the last hour since I saw him.

"Your guess is as good as mine."

"Get the scoop at lunch for me?"

"You bet I will. Can we have a rain check on lunch?"

"We can, but I need to get the details this afternoon! I'll stop by later." Carrie says as if we're back in middle school.

Get the scoop. Hmmm, if only it will be that easy...

Chapter 11

Realizing the impending hour, I locate a travel toothbrush in my cosmetic bag and a roll of floss. In seven years I have never brushed or flossed my teeth at work, but today is different. I apply a subtle hint of makeup so it doesn't look like as if I tried too hard, but also want to look a bit fresher.

As I apply the lip gloss, I am eye level with a family picture from Gran's refrigerator that I grabbed on my last walk through her house. It's from our last vacation to Bald Head Island with the four of us perched under a century-old oak tree. Matt and Graham stand tall in the back with Stella sitting on my knee in front. Our perfect little family is so handsome. Stella's petite frame and green eyes sparkle even in a photo. Years ago our hair would have had a similar golden blonde tint, but my routine coloring has given way to a darker shade. Graham and Matt have the same stature. Both having an athletic build, they look fit in anything they wear. Their dark blonde hair and crystal blue eyes are unmistakable. I remind myself that I couldn't have produced this amazing family with anyone other than Matt.

Again, startled by reality, I hear chimes from the front door.

"Be right there," I yell.

~

"Shit, be strong, Sam." I say this mantra at least three times to myself while taking a quick look in the mirror and tucking a stray hair behind my ear.

As I round the corner, I see Andy and a young lady standing at the counter.

"Hey," Andy says in a reserved tone never making eye contact with me.

He puts an arm around the girl standing beside him and gives her a good ole' pal kind of squeeze.

"I don't believe you met Anna when she ordered her dress a few days ago," he says without looking at her.

"Oh, nice to meet you," I mumble as I examine the youthful looking, barely college aged, cellulite free young woman. I feel completely sick inside. I had never pictured being a part of this moment and it does not feel good.

"Nice to meet you, Samantha. Carrie told me all about you."

"First of all, don't call me Samantha and second of all, don't talk about my best friend," I silently scream inside my head.

Anna almost runs to the size four dresses. Geez, could this get any freaking worse?

I am desperate for Carrie to show up anyway. She could save me from this mess. Maybe they won't notice if I quickly text her.

My breathing becomes labored as I work hard at taking deep breaths. In a flash, I feel miniscule and diminished in my own boutique.

As if Anna owns the place, she loudly announces, "I called Andy and he said he was in town to pick out his tuxedo so I just *had* to come. There's no way I'd let the biggest day of my life and my husband's fashion statement be left up to this guy."

Andy chuckles and rolls his eyes while Anna never misses a beat nearly pulling down the dresses as she spills over to the size two's.

I can tell she is not joking about the wedding being her biggest day because in her short twenty plus years, it was all about her. I realize my own cattiness and make a concerted effort to be neutral although it is killing me inside.

Anna takes a phone call from what sounds like her "BFF" and they talk for several minutes using acronyms like "OMG" and "LOL." Realizing his bride-to-be is going to be tied up for a few minutes, Andy asks me to show him men's formal wear.

As I lay the catalog on the table and watch him take a seat on the chaise, I tuck my hair behind my ears.

"You still play with your hair when you're nervous, I see."

"I'm not nervous. I just haven't had time to get a haircut," I announce with an annoyed tone, but know he is absolutely correct.

"You also still lie when you're nervous."

Andy says this obviously trying to get under my skin. And yes, he has succeeded.

Hearing this witty remark, I can't help but smile and sit next to him on the chaise. We look through the book, page by page. I attempt to do my job professionally by treating him like any other groom. While showing him the newest fashions and styles, I realize he is not listening to anything coming out of my mouth.

"I'm sorry, I know you're bored and would rather wait until Anna gets here," I say giving Andy an out.

"It's not that, it's just that I'm remembering when you told me your dream of owning your own wedding boutique. You used to correct me many times when I called it your "store." You always said that anyone could have a store, but you would have a fine boutique. Damn, look at what you've done."

I quickly look around to see if Anna is in earshot and thankfully she is still talking on her hot pink cell phone about Lord knows what.

"I can't believe you remember all of that. It's been so long ago," I whisper, but feeling like it was just yesterday.

Andy turns back to focus on me, closes the book, and reaches across to the stray piece of hair apparently just waiting for his attention. With a gentle swoop, he tucks it behind my ear.

"Samantha, those were your dreams, but they were ours at the time. Some things you just never, ever forget." The words flow from his lips as easily as ordering lunch.

As time nearly stops and fifteen years of memories hover like lead balloons in the air, Anna quickly rushes over to break up the moment.

"You guys act like you have known each other for years!" Anna says in her childish whine.

I shoot Andy a "what-in-the-hell" look and his eyebrows raise behind Anna's back as if to say, sorry.

"You know what, Anna, I need to get over to NC State and meet an associate in fifteen minutes, so we'd better reschedule."

"Annnndy, you *promised* me that you would take care of this. The wedding is less than six months away," Anna whines in her high pitched tone.

Desperate to ease the tension, I speak up and offer what I think is no less than brilliant.

"Anna, would you trust me to put your groom and groomsmen in something perfect for your wedding?"

With visible hesitancy, Anna finally agrees to my proposal which will get me out of having to be in this situation ever again.

"I'm going to give you both a business card with my work number, email and cell number. If you have any concerns, please call me."

I write my information on the cards and hand them to the pouty bride and seemingly flustered groom.

"Nice to meet you both," I convincingly say trying to keep up the fake façade and bid them both farewell.

Anna begins her rant before they even leave the store. Andy turns to look at me as and gives a half smile that was full of unspoken words and emotions. I can hardly look up without my eyes filling with tears.

After this ordeal, I decide to visit the Cupcake Shoppe and feed my emotions with a large red velvet cupcake piece of heaven. I lock the boutique door, savor each bite and replay the previous thirty minutes over and over in my head.

Why hadn't he told Anna who I am? Why was he attracted to such a young and seemingly trite bimbo? It is startling that he was able to recount the details of our hopes and dreams. Men are supposed to be callous and unforgiving. Plus, we parted on tense terms which should have made this "reunion" tense. Dammit, why is all of this happening and why now?

Chapter 12

Once again startled by my cell phone, I answer a call from Stella's teacher. Feeling as if I could crawl in a hole and not look back, I am glad I did not as this is an actual call that I need to take. According to Mrs. Emily, the two hundred fifty pound school nurse who still wears a white nursing outfit complete with tight white stockings, Stella is running a fever and needs to rest at home. I decide that after a hell of a day, I would take the last couple of hours of it to get Stella on the mend.

As I drive up to the front of the school, I see Stella and Mrs. Emily sitting on the steps engaged in deep conversation. Seeing Mrs. Emily for the first time in person, I can see why she has lines of students at her office every day for their various ailments. Her comforting body language and maternal physique would make even grown people feel better.

"Hey, sweetie. How are you feeling?"

"Hey, mommy. I am feeling okay, but I'm glad you're here."

Stella meets me halfway between the steps and the car with her Justin Bieber backpack engulfing her small frame.

"Thank you, Mrs. Emily. I really appreciate your care for Stella until I could get here," I say as I shake her hand.

"Not a problem. Stella's a dear. She was just telling me your ritual when she gets sick," Mrs. Emily says as she gives a wink in Stella's direction.

"Oh, really? What did you say, Stella?" I tickle her side to get a smile from her tightly drawn lips.

"You know, mommy. You tuck me tight in your bed, close the curtains, and make me as much macaroni and cheese that I want!"

"That's right, my dear. In fact, today is a perfect day to do it because daddy is out of town. Let's go in and call your brother to the office so we can get home to snuggle in the house."

"Thanks, Mrs. Emily!" Stella says with an earnest smile.

"You're welcome, Stella. Please get some rest," Mrs. Emily says as she looks back at us before taking the steps one-by-one.

The kids, Scarlet, Myrtle and I decide to watch our all time favorite show, Myth Busters, and drink hot chocolate. With Matt away at the art show for the next few days, we don't have to move a muscle. The timing is perfect for us to feast on mac and cheese and not leave the bed.

I had almost forgotten about the reconnection with my once dream man until I hear the "Glamorous" ring tone. Shit, Carrie is probably at *je t'aime* waiting to get an update.

"Hey sweetie. I am so sorry I forgot to tell you that I closed up early today because Stella's not feeling well. We decided with Matt gone that we'd snuggle together in bed."

"Not a problem and you know I understand. Tell her that her Aunt Carrie is hoping she feels better soon. Call me if I can help while Matt's out of town. Oh, by the way, there's a note taped to the door of the boutique."

"Weird – is it addressed to the boutique?" I ask calmly but hear my heart beating.

"It's hard to make out. I think it's Samantha Lynne. Pretty scribbled writing."

Within an instant, I know who it's from. That sentiment can only be from Matt, Carrie, Gran or Andy. Able to rule out three of them, I instantly know who it's from.

"Do you have your spare key with you?"

"Yep, I believe it's in my dash compartment."

"If so, can you set it on the front counter? I'll get it in the morning."

I do not want to risk it blowing away or getting picked up by someone else. Anymore drama right now would push me over the edge of what little sanity I have left. Even though Carrie is the only person I can trust to open it, I am not ready to go there with her just yet.

"Sure thing. I'm going in now. We'll chat tomorrow. Hope Stella feels better soon. Love you, mean it."

I smile as I remember Carrie saying "love you, mean it" since we were eight years old. As a kid you say words without really understanding their meaning. Over the last three decades, she and I have truly come to know what it means to care about one another through all of the ups and downs of life.

"Was that Aunt Carrie?" Stella asks.

"Yes, ma'am, she was calling to check on you," I say as I feel Stella's forehead and realize her fever is finally breaking.

~

The kids fall asleep on either side of me. Not being able to even turn over does not even bother me because the era of snuggling will begin to wane as the kid's age. There's a closeness I feel with them in the still of the night, and no matter what has transpired during the day, this quiet time with them is priceless.

My mind drifts as I think about seeing Andy again after so long. He has not changed one iota: tall, dark, and handsome with his same old southern charm. Gran had always liked Andy. He was very considerate to females and had nice manners, which of course, Gran adored.

While drifting off to sleep, I try thinking of my encounter with Andy as a beginning to an end. He had entered back into my life as abruptly as our afternoon ended. What did the note say? What more could he possibly want?

Secretly, I have always wondered what he was doing and now I know. Maybe I can finally put him to rest. Since Anna has given me permission to choose the tuxedos, I can get the wedding order wrapped up and let Carrie handle any specifics that may linger.

Our chance meeting was incredibly draining, yet frighteningly energizing. I realize I need to be focused on the present and not the past. This is easier said than done.

Chapter 13

I awake to the sounds of giggles from Stella and Graham. The two smiling faces are on either side of me with a finger almost touching each cheek hoping I'll turn quickly and get poked. Knowing their little trick, I pretend to stay asleep until they are distracted by Myrtle, then duck under the covers and begin my tickling attack. Glad the bed isn't empty with Matt away, I relish the time with the kids and reluctantly motivate the crew to get up and going.

While packing lunches, I see Gran's recipe box sitting on top of the stove. It sat on the seat beside me on the trek back to Raleigh as I did not want it to get lost in the shuffle of packing boxes. It was a last minute grab. With hardened cake batter on the top and sides, it is as if the recipes had just been used.

The recipe cards are priceless with Gran's familiar signature on the bottom of each card. "From the Kitchen of Ada" was neatly inscribed on the one-hundred plus cards with treasures from angel biscuits to her giblet gravy. With terms like pinches and dashes, it is not a stretch to picture her making each and every dish. Feeling like I want to reproduce every pone bread and ambrosia salad recipe in there, I decide there is no time like the present. Tonight will be "From the Kitchen of Ada" in Sam's kitchen!

Much to Graham and Stella's dismay, I drop them off in the "drive-thru" line at school. Why they despise being dropped off at the door to the school is a mystery to me. I know it sure beats riding the bus for hours each day. After answering twenty e-mails in the "drive-thru" line on my BlackBerry, I am exhausted even before beginning the day. With an overwhelming sense of urgency, I decide to make substantial changes in the way I deal with the daily schedule and demands.

Winding my way through the neighborhood back home, I see our neighbors running on the sidewalk. The wife flags me down to stop.

"Sam, Sam. Do you have a second?" Julie asks through pants.

"Sure. How are you all doing? Pretty morning for a run."

"We're good. We're doing just fine. Listen, Matt told me about your Gran and we are very sorry for your loss. Bless your sweet little heart. We really enjoyed seeing her the times she was in town and we'll certainly miss visiting with her, too. You doing okay?" Julie's husband, Tom, still running in place nods the entire conversation as if he's agreeing with her every word.

"Thank you. We're doing okay. I stayed back a couple of days to go through her things at the house. There's still work to do, but I was glad to have that time by myself there. Oh, thank you both for sending flowers. That meant a lot."

"You're welcome, dear. If we can help with the kids while Matt is out of town, please let us know. Looks like I better let Tom get back to his running. Talk to you soon, Sam!" Her words begin to trail as they continue their jog.

Watching my middle-aged neighbors take on the morning by getting out in nature and exercising makes me think back to when I ran with both Carrie and Matt. There was a sense of freedom and accomplishment to my days back then. And it hits me; I need to get back into running and regain that feeling and lifestyle. From this moment forward, I decide to take time for myself and start running again.

Even though it has been nearly a decade since I have run for any reason other than after the kids, I swing back by the house and decide there is no time like the present. Digging deep into the back of my closet, I finally locate my running shoes and slip them on. I also find my sports bra and squeeze my boobs into the decade old spandex. After two kids and twenty extra pounds, things have definitely shifted. I grab Graham's iPod, crank the volume, and head out the front door. Jogging at a good clip, I forget that I haven't pounded the pavement since I was pregnant with Graham. I decide not to push myself or my luck with the first run and head home after a mile. Feeling energized and centered, I shower and begin my day with renewed perspective. I grab Gran's recipe box and head out the door to *je t'aime* with an extra kick to my step.

Chapter 14

I have almost forgotten about my afternoon with Andy until I unlock the door and see the note Carrie placed on the counter. Touching it like it is an explosive device; I handle it with great care. Yep, this is from Andy alright. I would know his script anywhere. I open it to find two words – "I'm sorry." That's all it says; with no sign of who it is from, I still have no doubt of its sender.

I continue to remind myself that it was a random and meaningless encounter. I will complete the tuxedo order, have Anna sign off, and treat it like just another typical wedding. Feeling resigned to this plan, I get busy tying up loose ends. Before I have a chance to even wonder why I haven't heard from Matt, my cell phone rings with his voice on the other end.

"Hey stranger, what's going on?" Matt asks, not realizing the magnitude of the question.

"Long time since we talked, almost a whole day. Is the world coming to an end?" I tease trying to keep the conversation light.

"I hear ya. Good news, I've actually been slammed with the exhibition, but it's worth it. People are digging my collection. Sam, I think this is my best one yet."

"That's awesome! I am so proud of you. We're missing you though." I say with earnest.

His voice is so easy and familiar. Something I need to hear right now.

"I miss you guys, too. You still owe me, by the way, babe." It's nice to hear his flirty tone.

"I would have made good on my promise but you were good and asleep the other night, buddy. Good luck today and call us tonight so the kiddos can check in."

"Sure will. Love you, baby."

"Love you, too," I say as I see Carrie whipping around the corner in her BMW convertible.

I giggle as I think about Carrie and her first car. It, too, was a convertible, but it was literally a boat. Such a large car for such a small teenager, but it did spark her love for having the wind in her hair.

"Hey, honey, brought you breakfast. Are you eating and taking care of yourself?" Carrie interrogates me again with her motherly tone.

"Yes, mom. Actually, I am going to make a comfort food dinner that Gran would rearrange plans for if she were still alive. Wanna join us? Matt's out of town and the kids would love to see you, plus we can catch up."

"Good, country cooking with Sam flair, absolutely! But first, you HAVE to tell me about the mystery note! Please don't make me wait until dinner!"

"I was kinda hoping you'd forgotten about the note," I chuckle.

"Yeah, right. Never in this world!"

"It was just a note from Andy saying that he was sorry."

"Why was he sorry? Why did he feel like he had to leave you a note?" Carrie prods.

"He and Anna stopped by together to pick out his tux when he had said it would just be him," I casually say as if they are a typical bridal couple.

"*Shouldn't* they be together to choose the tuxedos, Sam?"

"They should, but it was obvious to me that he didn't *want* her there."

"Did *you* want her there?" Ouch. There it is. Carrie's question stopped my multi-tasking madness dead in its tracks.

"That's not a fair question. Carrie, I haven't seen him in years and if you want to know the truth, I wasn't ready to see him with someone else. So your answer is no."

"Well, I guess he did have reason to apologize. Does Matt know that Andy is in town?"

"Carrie, Matt doesn't even know who Andy is."

"Sam, be careful. Just be careful. You have a lot of emotions going on right now that can easily become intertwined with grief about Gran. We're going to need that wine tonight!"

~

Carrie joins us in the evening and contributes a large bottle of Riesling to the celebration of good food. Gran loved to eat but she was not much for alcohol. She wasn't necessarily opposed to it as long as young women did not embarrass themselves (or their families) in public. Gran and Papa always told me to watch out for boys, beer and dope. Those were the worst three things they feared for me. Ah, if life were only that simple now.

After being attacked by Scarlet, Myrtle, Graham and Stella, Carrie finally breaks loose to migrate to the kitchen where I have two wine glasses waiting. Sensing Carrie is unsettled from our earlier conversation about Andy, I wait for her questions to begin.

"Sam, you realize Andy's appearance was not due to chance, right?" she asks without really asking.

Quick to squelch simmering fires, I try and dismiss her instantly. "It is not even an issue because they won't be back until Anna comes to do her final fitting of the dress."

"I hear you, Sam, but I think you're being naïve. You have a rich history with Andy and you can't just put this away like you're folding clothes."

"You know I hate folding clothes and try to do it as little as possible."

"Sam, you know what I mean."

"I hear you, but I also know that I had to bury my feelings for him years after we lost touch and if I don't "put it away" as you say, I will begin to have what I dislike most - emotions and feelings that I may not be able to handle."

"All I'm saying is to take one day at a time..."

The four of us have a wonderful dinner with great food, superb wine and a prized friendship. Carrie keeps the kids hanging on her every word as she tells themstories of when we were young.

"Tell me another one, Aunt Carrie," Stella squeals.

"Okay, one last story before bedtime. In the summer, your mom and I used to stay up until midnight playing "flashlight tag" and "ghost in the graveyard."I would always know your mom was around because she would scream out of pure fright!"

"What Aunt Carrie isn't telling you is that she was screaming right beside me while holding on to my shirt so we wouldn't get separated. It takes a scaredy cat to know one," I kid.

"I wish we could play outside until midnight. Why can't we?" Graham says with a convincing tone.

"First of all, it's not the summer. Second of all, I don't think you can run around the neighborhood with flashlights all night or someone would call the police!" I motion them to follow me to their bedrooms so they can change their focus.

"That's not fair. You got to do it and you're fine," Graham retorts.

"That's disputable," Carrie says with a wink in my direction.

"We'll ask your dad when he gets back." After putting the responsibility on Matt, I pick Stella up from her chair and cradle her as if we were back in time. I struggle to carry her to her room, but manage as these moments are few and far between.

Graham shows Carrie his prized Star Wars action figures collection. I hear her falling for his ploy to stay up longer and rescue her from hours of battles between Luke and Darth Vader.

Finally able to relax, Carrie and I happily finish the bottle of wine. I decide to take the opportunity to convince Carrie that we should be running buddies. Having known each other for almost four decades, we have only worked out together for a brief stint in our twenties. Thinking Carrie will balk at my proposal, I have already planned a rebuttal.

Carrie shocks me with not even a futile attempt of opposition. "Fine, I'll do two days a week if we can run through downtown and Cameron Village."

With no shower at the boutique, I am wary of this plan but am willing to give it a try. I always keep toiletries around and since the hot, unbearable North Carolina temperatures have not yet arrived, I should be fine after a jog at least until July.

"Alrighty then, it's settled. Let's meet at the boutique tomorrow morning," I spit out quickly before she changes her mind.

"As long as we can have coffee after." Carrie says this as if it's her final demand.

"You know that's a yes. See you tomorrow and thank you for listening."

I wait for Carrie to say "Love ya, mean it," and she does.

Chapter 15

I eagerly curl up in bed with Myrtle on my pillow and Scarlet snoring beside the bed. The house is so peaceful. The kids are asleep so there's no extra noise for the first time all day. I had a good day, but wonder how the art show is going for Matt. Just as I pick up the phone to dial his number, my phone rings and it is him.

Instantly soothed by his voice, I listen to his excitement about how well his art show is going. People have flown in from all over the country to view his work. I can tell he is humbled by the turnout.

Due to the demand, he's decided to stay two extra days to tour the local art studios and talk with several potential business contacts. At first I am disappointed with his delay, but realize the time for working on his career is exactly what he needs. I also need time to focus on my end, too.

Just as I start to drift off to sleep, my phone rings with a text message. Not recognizing the number, I decide to read it in the morning. A few minutes later, it rings again with a second message from the same number. Annoyed with the disruption, I reluctantly check the phone to see who is texting so late at night. Shit, the number is unfamiliar, but the sender is not.

The first message reads: "Hey Sam. Sorry we couldn't chat the other day. Anna and I had different agendas. Andy."

I sit straight up in bed and remember I had given Anna and Andy my cell phone number in case they need me for a wedding emergency. I can't turn back now. I have to read the second message: "Could we have coffee tomorrow?"

Stunned, I wipe the sleep from my eyes and stare at the phone. I thought I had this tightly tucked away. Carrie is the one who is supposed to deal with the final wedding arrangements, which includes the two people I do not ever want to see together again. My plan has a kink. I did not anticipate he would actually use the number I gave him reserved only for wedding *emergencies*.

Should I ignore the texts and just have Carrie call Andy in the morning or should I text back and politely decline his offer for coffee?

I bury my head in the pillow and try to put it all away. Fifteen minutes creep by which feels like a lifetime. I decide a cup of coffee will help my decision or least be comforting for the moment so I make my way to the kitchen.

I reach for my favorite coffee cup that has slipped to the back of the cupboard. Using a step stool, I am easily able to grab the cup the kids made for me on Mother's Day when they were four and two years old. It would be forever dear to me because it was painted "Happee Moth's Day." I smile each and every time I use it. So it will not get broken, I use it only on special occasions. This is definitely a situation that calls for the "Moth" cup.

Liking things in their place, I immediately notice three boxes on the top shelf of which are definitely out of order and I begin remembering their origin. When Gran reluctantly moved to Raleigh, she brought several "treasures" to keep for the duration of her stay. With Gran's transition back to Fairfield after her three month stay, she asked us to keep the two pearl necklaces, six silver coins, and three shoe boxes. I placed the necklaces and coins in safe keeping while Matt took care of the boxes. I had forgotten about the boxes until this moment. I decide to pull down one of the boxes and take it and my cup of coffee to my bed against my better judgment.

Myrtle is very interested in the box contents and curls up in my lap waiting for my next move. I pull out letters thinking they are more of the same that I found in the Fairfield chest. Stacks of letters are tied with a satin bow with a decomposing dandelion tucked through the knot. My anticipation mounts as if I am opening a present – one that is so neatly wrapped and preserved.

Myrtle paws at the dangling ribbon, thinking it is a play toy. There is no way I can get the fur ball kitten to sleep now. No time like the present to see what other odd things Gran has saved.

The untied letters reveal a newspaper clipping that is wrapped in a perfect rectangle around the letters. When money was tight as a child, Gran taught me to wrap many a present in newspaper. On occasion I was lucky enough to have the colored comic page to help ease my embarrassment when presenting birthday gifts.

Thinking this newspaper is serving a similar purpose, I pause as I read the page title, "Local Professor Earns Top Honors at Oxford."

I reread the title which is sounding all too familiar. Knowing this is surely a coincidence, I skip to the middle of the two page spread to confirm the fluke but instead read the following:

> Andy Latimer describes this experience as being the chance
> of a lifetime. "The opportunity to immerse myself in such
> a rich educational and cultural environment will have

*long lasting positive effects. I plan to return to the East
Carolina University community as an Assistant Professor
in the Philosophy department. This immersion experience
will ensure my dedication to lifelong learning for both me
and my students."*

Without a doubt, these words are Andy's. This is definitely
the smart and charming Andy who even proves himself on a different
continent. This was *my* Andy whom I sent to Oxford.

Damn, what happened to the simple life - a life where Gran
just nodded her head in passive aggressive disagreement? Fast as I
can, I nearly rip open the first letter I see in the stack. The first letter
is postmarked 1992. I quickly glance at the next ten envelopes and
again, they are all postmarked 1992. How could I forget 1992? That
was my first year at UNC and Andy was finishing his degree overseas
in England. Shaking uncontrollably, I open the first letter and cannot
believe my eyes.

Dear Gran,

*I hope you remember me. I am Andy, Sam's
friend, and we met several times when we came to Fairfield
to take you to church. I am finishing my advanced degree
in Philosophy at Oxford University.*

*Because of logistics, I do not hear from Sam very
often. In fact, I have reached out to her several times and
have had no communication in return.*

*I was hoping to write to you to make sure she is
okay. I don't need to know specifics, but I would like to
know nothing is wrong. I care for her deeply and only want
the best for her.*

*I hope to hear from you soon. Please send her my
love when you talk with her.*

Fondly,
Andy

Feeling breathless and light headed, I try with all my soul to
understand what I am reading. I hold in my shaking hands dozens of
letters from Andy to Gran that have been waiting for me for almost
twenty years. My head spins with emotions of both hurt and anger. I
am at a loss for words.

Why am I just now reading these words? Letter after letter

affirming Andy's compassion for me and I am seeing them now for the first time? Then I remember. I nearly choke as I remember why I had never seen them.

~

This memory is way too easy to recall even though I had buried it deep into my soul. During the spring semester of my freshman year at UNC, I had lunch with a classmate from my economics class who had been catching my eye. Deciding we would study together and perhaps spark a little romance on the side, we made our way back to Granville Towers dorm.

Seated stoically on the bench outside of my residence hall was Gran. I could not believe my eyes with my first thought being something was wrong. She had driven, for the first time in her life, west of Greenville without anyone else in the car. Gran assured me there was not an emergency which calmed my fears, but definitely sparked my curiosity.

I quickly introduced her to my friend, Jason, and then took a moment to cut the afternoon short with my cute studying partner. While Gran went to retrieve a package from her car, I gave Jason a kiss which made him want to come back later and finish what we started.

I helped Gran with a large package and headed upstairs to my room. Always to the point, Gran wasted no time in revealing the contents of the package as she wanted to head back home that afternoon before dark. She sat down on the bed and patted an empty space beside her for me to sit. She reached into the box and pulled out a letter and handed it to me. My first thought was that she been out of stamps for months and had saved her correspondence and decided to hand deliver them all.

I began to read the first letter and my heart fell. It was a letter from Andy. My hands began to tremble. Not being able to see straight, I immediately threw it on the floor and started to cry like I had never cried before.

Gran placed the letter on the floor and reached into the box only to produce two dozen more. Not believing my eyes, I could not emotionally and physically take reading another word that his hand had written. I could literally taste the hurt and pain.

Almost unable to speak I was finally able to whisper, "Gran, he was the one who left me. Andy was the one who left the country."

Wiping continuous tears from my cheek, I did not give her a chance to contest.

"Gran, I seriously can't take this. He can't have it both ways.

I have always tried to make my own way and I can't do that when he wants me to live vicariously through him in another continent. Please, please, don't show me another one."

Gran placed her worn hand on my heart and said with the most tenderness she had ever shown, "Honey, you will always make your way. I realize I don't understand the root of your hurt. But I do know your heart and I also know that you have closed it to him. Just know that your path in this life has room for two."

Gran packed up the surprise package, and, as quickly as she came, she was gone.

~

Thankfully my roommate was gone for the weekend. I locked the door and cried until I had no tears left. The weekend was a blur as I don't remember eating, showering, or doing anything else other than hiding under my covers.

Stubborn as stubborn could be, I finally decided that I had to get out of my stupor. I realized I couldn't be mad with Gran for bringing letters from the man Gran knew I would always love. Gran had no clue why Andy was reaching out to me to make sure I was okay.

I had buried all of those memories until that moment as I relived them alone in the dorm room. All of the memories flooded my entire body and soul. The vivid memories surfaced too easily for my good: our last weekend together, the doctor's appointments, the excitement, the fear, and the losses.

~

For our last weekend together before Andy's departure to England, we took a weekend trip to Asheville and literally locked ourselves in a rustic mountain cottage. It was our first weekend together truly on our own. I certainly had no idea it would be our last. Excited to be out of our normal routine, we made a pledge to stay at the cottage all weekend. We visited the local grocer to stock up on kitchen necessities.

Not that the place was plush in any stretch of the imagination, but it was a palace to us. We could be mindless with our time as there were no schedules to be adhered to for three days. The only agenda we had was eating something every now and then, hiking through paths surrounded by rhododendron and playing in the hot tub.

The first night set the tone for our entire weekend. After I finished a bath in a white porcelain claw foot tub, I made my way through the three room house towards the kitchen. All I could see were the stars glowing in the jet black mountain sky and the soft glow of candlelight. The scene was perfect. Dozens of candles, all soft white with the fragrance of gardenia, were strategically placed.

As I slowly made my way towards the glow, I felt what seemed like velvet cradling my toes. Surprisingly undisturbed, I glanced toward the floor only to discover hundreds of rose petals. Between the scent of gardenias and fresh roses, I was already headed to complete and utter ecstasy.

Not seeing Andy anywhere, but knowing he was orchestrating the event, my excitement mounted. I tiptoed into the dining room and turned back towards the door. I gasped as I felt two hands rest on my hips. His strong hands spun me eagerly but gently toward him. Suddenly I was face to face with the man I loved, desired, and respected. He was sitting confidently at the dining room table surrounded by chocolates of all different shapes and sizes.

As he stood to greet me with a knee buckling kiss, I realized all he had on was an apron. Sensing my eagerness to go straight for making our own heat in the kitchen, he quickly handed me a box to slow me down.

Inside was a matching apron, except a hell of a lot skimpier. Wasting no time, I stripped down and slipped the apron over my chest revealing the tops of my thighs. I sat down on Andy's lap where we began to savor chocolate covered strawberries, truffles, and everything else imaginable.

Andy began dipping his finger in the chocolate and swirling it on my chest and thighs. In an instant, he cleared off the table and positioned me on top of the red tablecloth where he began tasting the chocolate. He slowly licked every inch of dark and white chocolate from my nipples down to my inner thighs.

Totally unconcerned with where we were, it seemed only sensible that the dining room was turned into our room of delight. I pushed him back, sat on top of his lap and slowly began making love to him in the dark with only the glow of candlelight.

For three days, we wore nothing but our aprons. The only schedule we kept was making love morning, noon, and night. Our love was both tender and passionate. He knew me like no one else ever would. He could ravage my body, but also knew what made me tick which made him even sexier.

We both dreaded the end to a perfect weekend. On Sunday afternoon, the drive back to Chapel Hill went way too quickly. I yearned for the tires to go flat or my appendix to erupt – anything to stop time.

We said our goodbyes and like that, Andy left for another country.

~

     Initially, our communication was frequent, but that soon tapered off as Andy became immersed in his studies. Dealing with the scheduling of calls with different time zones became tiresome, too. Caught up in acclimating to a new year at UNC, the time flew for me. I was so busy for a while that I did not even realize I had gone two months without a period. I first thought its absence was due to stress. A new city, new school, no Andy – a lot had been going on. My better judgment kicked in and I realized I needed to attend to my health.

     Terrified, I visited the campus health clinic for a pregnancy test. Sure enough, it was positive. After nearly fainting in the tiny room on the brown leather table, I immediately picked up the phone to call Andy. Because of the time difference, I was unable to reach him which forced me to leave a panic stricken message with very vague facts.

     "Hey Andy, I know you are probably in class all day, but I really need to talk to you. Please call me no matter what time it is. Love you."

     Days and weeks went by and I heard nothing. The man I had created a baby with had left my life and country and I was completely on my own. I absolutely could not tell Gran because good girls definitely didn't have sex before marriage, and certainly didn't get "that way" as she called it before marriage either.

~

     Alone and scared, I confided in my best friend, Carrie. Besides Andy, Carrie truly knew my heart and soul. She knew without debate that an abortion was not an option for me. We weighed the pros and cons of keeping the baby and the cons clearly outweighed the pros, but it was still no contest to me.

     I had to keep the baby. It was one of the only things that would remind me of Andy and the love we shared. I rationalized every possible scenario of getting through it alone. I talked myself into hiding the pregnancy from Gran by not traveling to Fairfield the last few months of the third trimester. Plus, Gran was always saying I was too thin, so she would be pleased if I had added a few extra pounds. The typical freshman fifteen would be easily justified. Once I really began to show, it would be mid-spring and the semester would be almost over.

     "One step at a time," Carrie kept telling me.

Once I made my mind up about something, there was no stopping me. However, the first step was to make a doctor's appointment and get healthy.

The due date was circled with a huge heart on my dorm room calendar. The date was arbitrary to anyone looking at it, but I knew what it signified and that was all that mattered. Carrie called every day to check on me. Like clockwork, she also asked me if I wanted her to call Andy again.

Each and every time I quickly responded a firm no, but in my heart, I meant yes. The last few days he and I had shared were unlike anything I had ever experienced and ever would. From our love a baby was formed and I wasn't able to share it with him. It tore my heart apart.

Fifteen weeks into the pregnancy, I began to cramp during chemistry lab. The pain was so intense I had to brace myself on the table. I made my way to the restroom where I discovered blood. Along with the blood, my tears began to flow and would not stop. I tiptoed hunched over across campus finally making it to the infirmary where the doctor gave me an exam which confirmed a miscarriage.

I could not get out of the building fast enough. Not wanting to believe the result, I was seen for an emergency appointment at the obstetrician's office. Sadly, an ultrasound confirmed the previous test results. Again, it showed no heart beat or sign of a fetus. The pain I felt was so great that it felt as if a piece of me had died, too.

~

Knowing the toll the ordeal had taken on my body and soul, Carrie invited me to go to Hawaii for the holidays with her family. This was her very unselfish attempt to help ease the pain. She was right. The warm sun and sand did help me recover physically, but emotionally, my heart was still torn to shreds.

Getting back into the swing of things after the holiday break was not easy. However, typical to my personality, I quickly learned how to stand on my own two feet. Doing so took more guts and courage than I ever thought was possible. When I returned to my dorm, dozens of messages from Andy lit up the answering machine. Much to my utter shock, he had come back to the United States for a surprise visit between semesters. We had missed one another by a mere twenty-four hours. I had learned to forget about the man who had forgotten me when Andy unexpectedly reintroduced himself back into my life.

Of course he did not just come and go; he left a package for me on his way back to the airport. It was a perfectly wrapped small package. The paper was a gorgeous lavender wrap with foil imprints of what looked to be a royal crest. Methodically, I carefully removed each millimeter of tape in order to preserve the last tangible item Andy had touched. With the wrapping removed, a small box was revealed. Upon further examination I see a red felt box. I held it in a tight grasp for several minutes before opening the dainty box.

With absolute care, I opened the box to find a crystal heart necklace that took my breath away. A colorful brochure indicated the treasure was from a museum in Vienna. Tucked neatly under the jewelry was a note that I was frightened to open but desperately wanted to read.

Dear Sam,

I have been trying to call you for the past couple of weeks but have not been able to reach you. I called Gran and she told me you were vacationing with Carrie. I should have called you before I left, but I wanted to surprise you. Guess that didn't work out so well.

Several weeks into my time at Oxford I was asked to travel to Vienna to spend the semester studying with guest lecturers. I enjoyed it immensely and had mentoring from many great minds.

The downfall was that I lived with a family during the semester who had no phone so I had to always try and call from a pay phone. I tried many times but always seemed to get your answering machine. When I did get through to leave you messages, I never heard back.

I have missed talking to you more than you'll ever know. Maybe you could come during Spring Break? I will be back at Oxford starting tomorrow and will be back in my own room with a phone.

I hope you like my gift. It is a small token in comparison of my feelings for you. I found it in a Vienna garden shop that overlooked the most beautiful garden. I wanted you by my side to experience it with me. I hope you will wear it and think of me.

Merry Christmas and I love you. Andy

At that moment, I realized Andy had never received my messages and did as soon as he returned to his dorm room at Oxford. My heart sank. I had spent months thinking he had moved on and did not care. Jesus, he had now returned to his world in England to hear my cry for help.

However, my cries had changed over time. I had to pick myself out of the gutter so many times the past few months, and as a result, I became self-sufficient with my emotions and pain. To my detriment, I had chosen to go through it all with just Carrie by my side. Over the last couple of months, I had closed that chapter of my life and didn't think I could go back and poke the fire ever again.

Everyday, the phone would ring and I would wait for the answering machine to pick up. Andy called dozens of times upon his return to Oxford and I would listen to each message and double over from the pain in my heart. Instead of reaching back out to Andy, I sealed those memories tightly and did everything I could to move on.

~

It was so apparent that Gran had not known any of the hell between us. Andy obviously was reaching out to my grandmother to see if I was in fact, okay. She was merely trying to help. After four months of letters from Andy and knowing I was not myself, she loved me enough to get in the car and drive hours from home to lay her eyes on me. She fulfilled her purpose, said her piece and drove back home.

Still stubborn as a damn mule, I could not open my heart. The suffering had closed the door to what I thought would be forever.

~

More than fifteen years later, the letters still tear my heart wide open. Andy had poured out his heart and soul in each and every one. Gran had been the caretaker of these precious words for all of these years. Why had she kept all the letters? Why did she bring them to Raleigh except to hope that I would discover the contents?

Completely overwhelmed with the love and heartfelt compassion Andy had expressed and not caring that the clock has moved past midnight, I pull out another stack of envelopes and begin reading more of the same. The postmark dates on the envelopes vary, but no years were missing from 1993 to 2009.

My breathing shallows as I realize Andy had continued to keep in touch with Gran. My chest pounds, making breathing a chore. One by one, I open them all in sequential order, reading letter after letter asking about me. Andy kept Gran attuned to his professional progress by sending articles he had clipped from his published journals. I even found the boutique announcement from the News and Observer. Feeling overwhelmed and shocked that Andy has unknowingly been a part of my life for years, I start to mentally record hundreds of questions for him.

Everything that previously seemed so solid in my life is now on shaky ground. The reconnection with Andy had not been random. He hadn't disappeared – he has always been right here. Gran had respected my wish to let the past be the past, but how could she have kept it going for so long? Had Gran been waiting for Matt and me to fall apart to interject these life changing reminders?

Wearily, I look at the clock and am unsurprised that it is well after 2am. I struggle with texting Andy back so late. What if he is with Anna? Feeling utterly overwhelmed, I decide to call the one person who will know what to do, Carrie.

"Sam, are the kids ok? Are you okay?"

"Hey sweetie. Yes, yes, they are and so am I. I'm so sorry for calling so late but I really need to talk."

"Sure, what's going on?" Carrie inquires in a half awake tone.

I spill it all to Carrie. From the box of letters to the evening's text messages, I recount every little detail. Carrie, fully awake now, is listening to each and every word. I can tell she is listening to the facts but I also feel that she is listening to my voice. The tone of it is different than it has been in years.

"Sam, I think you need to try and sleep for the next few hours until the kids wake up."

"Sleep? Sleep? I don't think that's possible!"

"Sam, don't text Andy this late at night. It will be morning soon enough. Please, please try and keep yourself going physically so that you can be strong emotionally."

"What do I do in the morning?"

"Don't worry about tomorrow today. Get through the night. Don't forget that we're running after the kids go to school, so we'll have some time to talk. I promise."

"I hate when you put it back on me."

"Don't I know that! You answer all of my shitty problems. I know that you have the answers. You just may not know it yet."

"Thank you for being here for me, Carrie."

"Where else would I be at two in the morning, missy? Seriously, Sam, you don't ask for help very often, so when you do, I listen."

"Love you, mean it, and see you in the morning." Wow, I actually beat Carrie to her own line.

Drifting to sleep is easier than I anticipate. Myrtle claims her space on top of my head while Scarlet sighs as if to say, "Finally, you're going to sleep."

Unable to recall one thing I dreamt due to total exhaustion, I wake up extremely rested and take the extra few minutes of quiet to gather myself for the day. After the coffee begins to brew, I curl up beside the gas logs to get warm. Looking around the room, I see the home Matt and I have lovingly created a home built around a shared bond.

In a split second, doubt creeps its way back in. Is my time spent running in a million directions to try to conceal the emptiness I could be hiding? Matt and the kids seem happy and fulfilled, but are they? I couldn't be mad at Andy for not telling Anna about our relationship because I certainly have never told Matt about Andy, the pregnancy and my extreme regret about losing him. Both Andy and I have kept our secret pain buried.

I gather the letters and place them back into Gran's box before Stella and Graham awake.

Chapter 16

The morning launches into the normal rush. Feeling like I want, no need, to do things differently today, I decide the three of us would have breakfast out instead of the same old cereal. Plus, I was ready to get the day started.

Stella is extremely chatty due to the excitement of "bring your pet to school" day. Her begging to bring Myrtle to show off has been utterly relentless. Even though I am very hesitant to bring such a young animal to school to be handled by dozens of kids, I know it is important to Stella. So, during the last few minutes of show and tell, I will be a good mom and bring the newest family addition to school.

After dropping the kids through the "drive-thru" line, I head straight to the boutique. Thinking Carrie has good reason to stand me up since I interrupted her sleep, I am prepared to run alone. Much to my surprise, Carrie is already there in her running gear waiting for me on the bench.

"Damn, it is freezing out here. Whose idea was this anyway?"

"Sam, I am a little groggy this morning because SOMEONE woke me up. I could easily crawl back in the bed, so don't tempt me!"

Not to waste time, we take off for a jog around Cameron Village. We circle the perimeter once and decide that since we are still alive without a lung collapse, we run towards NC State. We not only easily pass the Bell Tower, we end up continuing towards Pullen Park. Even though I am a Carolina girl, I dearly love Raleigh and feel extremely connected to the area because of its proximity to *je t'aime*.

Nearly out of breath, we take a break and rest on the park swings.

"Do you remember how we used to swing for hours and hours? Never getting bored of it or wondering what we were going to do next?"

"I do. Those were simple times, dear." I hear a hint of nostalgia in Carrie's voice.

"Those were times when we were being looked after. Someone always had their eye on us." Just as I comment, I watch a mom keeping one hand on her toddler while keeping an eye on her four year-old hellion throwing sand.

"You know what's crazy, Sam?"

"Yes, lots of things, but what this time?"

"It's insane that we do not give ourselves what we need. We don't take the time for us as individuals anymore."

"You're absolutely right. If we don't take care of ourselves, no one else will. That is for sure!"

"So, what are you going to do about seeing Andy?"

I knew this question was coming, but didn't know when.

"Well, it seems as if I can't avoid him because he knows where I work and is texting me now, so it's probably pointless to pretend he doesn't exist."

"Why Sam, that is progress for you, my dear. Not avoiding this is something I did not expect from you. So maybe you don't need me as your friend anymore!"

"Now you know one of the ONLY reasons I am where I am today is because of you. So no, you're not off the hook that easily!" I tease and twirl her swing.

"Seriously, though, I just don't know. This has all hit me so fast; I want to be careful and thoughtful in my steps."

"Then I think you have your answer – day by day."

"Sam, can we walk for a couple of blocks. I am feeling this run in my shins."

"Of course." I do not dispute her wishes and am glad as I feel heavy after our discussion.

It's obvious we're both deep in thought over our intense exchange. Our friendship works because we can lay everything out on the table, push one another's buttons, and know when to back off when we're too close to the edge.

Knowing Carrie almost thirty five years helps our well-oiled friendship run smoothly, but the longevity is just a piece of it. I like to be with her and want to spend time together. It's automatic for me to trust what she says as I don't believe there to be one self-serving bone in her body.

~

Even though Carrie is not married with responsibilities of her own family, she is wise beyond her years. Her spirit was tested years ago when her fiancé, Josh, was killed in the Iraqi war. They met in Boone at Murphy's where she waited tables to help pay her way through college. They had a fast but passionate love affair during her last semester. Josh was enjoying what he thought was a permanent leave from the army when he got orders that he would be heading back to Iraq in six months. Carrie graduated from Appalachian State a week after the announcement and the two immediately left the country to spend the remaining months backpacking through Europe. They got to know one another in a way very few couples have a chance to experience. By spending days and nights together in foreign places and using survival tactics in many cases, their dependence on one another grew rapidly.

Lucky enough to spend time with them in Italy while on a bridal buying trip, I was blessed to be in their company and watched them interact as if they had been married for fifty years. Their connection was solid and their physical chemistry was over the top, too. Days before their departure back to the United States and Josh's departure to Iraq, he proposed to Carrie at the top of the Eiffel Tower. Promising their commitment to one another at the top of the tower in the most beautiful city in the world made them feel indestructible.

~

Assuming Josh would be gone for only six months during his tour of duty, Carrie began planning a wedding to coincide with his return. Just two months later, Carrie received the call no one ever wants to hear. While I was on the road home from a trip to Boston, she called me with news that is frozen in time. Driving through the countryside of West Virginia, I found Carrie's voice almost inaudible through the nooks and crannies of the desolate mountains.

"Hello?"

"Sam, Sam, where are you?" Carrie frantically screamed into the phone.

"Sweetie, I'm in West Virginia and my cell strength is not very good. What's wrong? Are you okay?"

The signal strength faded as I heard her screaming through tears, "Sam, he's dead!"

"Oh God."

Repeating those two words aloud for miles and miles, I eagerly waited for a signal to reappear on the phone. My best friend's heart was shattering in thousands of pieces and I knew I had to get to her. Seven hours later, I finally reached her.

Arriving at her apartment with tires screeching at eight in the morning, I let myself in her apartment with an extra key she had shared. I found her curled in a ball asleep on the sofa, an empty box of tissues and a photo album resting in her arms. Desperately wanting to keep from disturbing her, I lifted the album from her hand and flipped through its contents. Pages of photos documenting their time together were the only thing remaining of their love.

Grabbing an afghan that Gran made for Carrie's high school graduation, I gently draped it over her legs careful not to awake her. Utterly exhausted but thankful she was not alone any longer; I fell asleep at Carrie's feet.

When we both awoke, the only thing that made sense was to let her cry. Carrie and Josh had been looking forward to meeting one another's families and sharing their engagement.

"I feel like this is all a dream. Sam, we fell in love so quickly, but it was real. It was the only thing that I've ever been sure of."

Thankful for the time I shared with them in Italy, I grieved with her for her loss and devastation. Several months passed, and her hurt began to turn into hollow grief. Even though Carrie and I would try to keep the memories alive, it just wasn't enough.

Late on a Thursday night, Carrie called me and said to pack my bags. An hour later, we raced to Boone to the first place she and Josh met, Murphy's Restaurant and Bar. Naturally, Murphy's was our first and last stop of the trip. Carrie had called several of her friends who were art majors to meet us. With hundreds of photos from their travels, the friends were able to picture the two and their adventures in life and love.

Working through the night, the friends transferred the memories from paper to a brick wall that instantly became a magical mural. The interpretation of their boat ride down the Seine to the lights on the top of the Eiffel Tower, their time spent together was forever captured. Spanning more than ninety feet in length, it was breathtaking both in its artistry and meaning.

Every time someone passed the artists busy at work, Carrie was able to tell her story again which made it real and kept Josh alive in her heart. She was finally able to give their love the attention it deserved.

Since 1994, Carrie has gone back to Boone on the anniversary of the night she and Josh met to have a drink for the two of them. Local artists have kept the mural in pristine vibrancy through the years. It's become a tourist and local community attraction.

Chapter 17

We decide to run the last half mile and break the silence by laughing about the last time we exercised together. I clearly remember it like it was yesterday. It was a brisk November morning and I was thirty eight weeks pregnant with Graham. Matt and I had gone for our weekly OB checkup that morning to find that my body was not progressing towards having the baby. The physician suggested doing some extra exercise like walking or heaven forbid, having sex. Matt was all for the latter option, but it didn't make sense to me that we would do the same thing to put me in labor that we did to get me pregnant! In an easy choice in my mind, Carrie and I took to walking the baby out. After our third lap around Cameron Village, I slowed to salivate over the winter window fashions at SoHo. Lost in a moment of wondering if my basketball sized belly would ever again fit in anything other than a XXL sized jersey, the feeling of cool water running down my leg snapped me back into reality.

"Oh my God, Carrie! This is it. My water has actually broken on its own!"

She and I danced down the brick sidewalks of Cameron Village thinking the baby was on its way! As Carrie hugged me and dropped her hands to my stomach, she noticed my water bottle, which was attached to a fanny pack on my waist, turned upside down with water dripping from its lip.

"Sam, honey, I hate to tell you this, but I think your water bottle tipped over and caused the wetness. Unless, of course, you drank an entire bottle of water while I wasn't looking." Carrie said this while handing me the dry-as-a-bone water bottle.

"Well, shit." I say as I sit down on the nearest park bench.

"We tried. We'll keep trying every day," Carrie says with optimism.

"Matt may have his wish of getting this baby out his way."

"Well, we do know he can't stay in there forever," Carrie says as I waddle back to *je t'aime*.

Turns out, Graham did almost stay in my warm uterine oven

for what seemed like forever. He was two weeks to the day late. Even after all the walking, and yes, sex, Graham had a mind of his own. His stubborn entry into the world was a great indication of what his little personality would bring.

~

As we slow our pace and make the final leg to the boutique, Carrie slows to a stop. I look over at her to see her gaze locked on *je t'aime*. Carrie's light hearted tone from our false labor story suddenly turns to stone. I follow her gaze and quickly reflect the same concern.

~

There he is – Andy – sitting on the same wrought iron bench where I have sat many times when I needed some quiet time to reflect. My mind starts racing.

"God, I look terrible. What do I say? I'm not ready to have the conversations I need to have with him."

"I could hear you two laughing a half mile away," Andy says as he gives Carrie a hug.

"Long time, Andy, great to see you."

"Well, I need to get back and have a shower before my first client, so tootles." Carrie is obviously hurrying to get out of this scene.

Damn, she's leaving us. We won't be able to fill the time with typical fake conversation you end up having with people you haven't seen in a while. As Carrie speeds away in her fashionable car, I grab my garment bag from the back bench seat of my van. Thankfully I have packed a change of clothes.

With nervous hands, I am unable to steady the keys long enough to insert it into the lock. Within seconds, my keys drop to the ground. Reaching down, I pick them up with one hand and tuck a strand of hair behind my ear with the other. I notice Andy smiling and know exactly why.

Why does he have to know me so freaking well? I can't even disguise my nervousness around him because he sees right through it. I consciously try to control my nerves.

He helps me with my bag as I unlock the door and flip on the lights. It's almost surreal to me as it feels like we're walking into our home together.

"Andy, I hate that I look so rough. Carrie and I had made this our first running date and had not planned on having any visitors." I say this to break the silence, but also to explain my appearance.

"Sam, first of all, I'm not a visitor. Secondly, you do not need to make excuses, you look great."

As I reach for my duffle bag to change clothes, he grabs my hand and stutters.

"I, I am sorry for just showing up here, Sam. I sent you the texts last night and I feel really bad for bothering you. I wanted to apologize in person."

"You don't need to make excuses, either." There, back at you.

"I'll be back in a minute," I announce as I make my way to the storage area to do a Wonder Woman transformation.

"Sam, I'm going to run up to the coffee shop and get a couple of cups for us. Be back in a minute."

"Oh, you know what? How about taking the keys and locking me in when you leave?"

"Sure will. Where are they?"

"Oh, they're back here," I yell as I turn to pull them from my purse.

I can see Andy through the slits of the curtains that separate the storage area from the showroom. I stare at his tall, sturdy and handsome profile for several seconds before tossing him the keys. With a fast swoop of his arm, he catches the keys effortlessly.

"See you in a sec."

Of all the days with no shower – sweaty and red faced. I use his absence to make a quick call to Carrie to build my confidence.

"Carrie, Jesus, what in the hell do I do now?"

"Sam, honey, you are going to be fine. Breathe and talk to him. You have known him forever. He is not a stranger to you."

"I know. You're right. Am I going to hell?" I jokingly ask but not wanting to know the answer.

"Babe, no. Plus, if you do, we'll be going together!"

"I just arrived home to get a shower. I'm here if you need me and I promise we'll talk later. Love you, and love yourself, Sam."Oh my goodness, Carrie altered her usual closing. That's huge as I take note of her last words.

~

With the clock ticking, I get back to the task at hand which is to get rid of my exhausted and sweaty look. Stripping my shoes, stretch pants, shirt and sports bra, I look at myself in the mirror almost naked. It is the first time I've done so in a long time. My usual habit is to rush from the shower and slip on an outfit in under five minutes. I turn to the side and look at my profile; while I am thicker in the

middle and my breasts are not as perky as they once were, I actually
feel decent about myself.

Thankfully, the packed pencil skirt is not too wrinkled. In
the rush of the morning, I was also glad I had not forgotten to pack
another bra. The black lace push-up bra sure beats the racer back
sports bra that barely fits.

I hear the front door chimes and know Andy has returned.
Realizing I need to speed up my dressing efforts, I reach for my red
cashmere v-neck sweater. As I stand to slip it over my head, I jump
as I see Andy standing in the storeroom doorway with the keys held
straight out towards me. Flustered, I quickly pull the sweater over my
head and through my arms.

"Nice try," Andy snickers as he looks down at my sweater.

"Shit. That's what I get for trying so hard."

With utter embarrassment heating my face, I see the tag
sticking out of the front and realize my sweater is on backwards. I am
certain my cheek color matches the color of my sweater.

I slip my arms out and begin turning my sweater around as
Andy reaches towards me.

"Here, let me help."

Without pause, Andy smoothes the fabric around my waist.

"I don't know why you're so nervous, Sam."

"Oh, I don't know either. It's definitely not due to the fact that
you just saw me half-naked!"

"Not like I haven't seen it before."

This is not good. His flirty remarks and damn cute looks are
going to send me over the edge. I have to keep my cool. I am not the
young girl he used to make swoon. I am a grown, married woman,
mother of two, and successful business owner. I cannot let myself go
where it wants to go.

"You got me with that one. But, I think we can say it's not
quite the same. This body is definitely different because it sure does
not look like it did almost twenty years ago."

Okay, now I'm immediately regretting my pseudo-flirty tone.

"I see you're still having to work on your self-confidence."

God, have I not changed one iota in the last twenty years?!

"Seriously, here are your keys. Sorry I put you in an *awkward*
position," he says with a wink and an almost confident smile.

"I hope you know that you have no reason to be nervous or
embarrassed around me, Sam. You do know that, right?"

"I know, it's just that…"

"We've done nothing wrong here. It's just like you helping
someone try on their formal wear. No different."

Yeah, right. No different.

~

Realizing I need a moment to gather myself, Andy walks through the curtain to the showroom. I look around the boutique and am proud to have him here. The space is sizable and the colors are warm. Even the storage room is inviting. The curtain that shelters the storage room is a beautiful floral pattern in a heavy silk fabric which coordinates with the dressing room material.

I feel like my work has paid off at *je t'aime*. I built my dream from the ground up and am proud of the fruits of my labor.

Once again, I can see Andy through the curtain. He's placed his hat on backwards and is sipping his coffee taking care to look around. His muscles flex as he pulls the cup to his lips.

"Damn, this is not fair, just not fair," I say quietly to myself.

Have I focused too much on this business instead of my needs in my personal life? No matter what, I like who I am at this moment, and, as Carrie said, we have to take care of ourselves. Here I go...

Andy turns abruptly towards me as if he is in deep thought as well.

"Coffee, just what I need, especially this morning."

"I think it's just the way you like it. Light cream and sugar?" He shows no lack of confidence in his efforts.

"Actually, I think you missed it slightly. It's light sugar and cream."

Not having an immediate comeback, he plays with the lid of the cup.

"Seriously, thank you very much."

"You're welcome," he says while reaching in his pocket for his cell phone.

I give him privacy to answer his call but stay within ear's reach to hear the details.

"Hello?"

"Oh yes, hello Dr. Turner, I'm doing fine and hope you are."

"Sure, I'll call you Richard."

"Yes, I'm still in town."

Only hearing one side of the conversation is grueling as I try to connect the puzzle pieces.

"I'd love to have dinner. That place is near my hotel. I can just meet you there."

What the heck, near his hotel? Is he not staying with Anna?

"Six-thirty sounds great."

"Uh, no, it will just be me. Thanks for the invitation and I'll look forward to seeing you and your wife."

Obviously startled by the call, he takes a moment to put away his phone.

I busily pretend to rearrange a bridesmaids gown with one hand while I sip my liquid drug with the other. Not hearing Andy's movement for a few moments, I turn to locate him. As I do, I run smack into his chest. The steaming hot coffee splatters between us soaking our shirts. Neither of us moves away from the scalding burn of the coffee. The heat between our bodies feels good, too good.

"Sam, are you okay?"

Still not moving I just nod my head. With his hands free he takes my sweater and pulls it away from my chest revealing a completely soaked body.

My eyes now level with his chest, I am eye to eye with his protruding muscles peeking through his coffee drenched shirt. I reach up and lay my hand on the soaked oxford.

Andy's gaze does not leave my saturated sweater as he sighs, unaware that I hear him. The silence is heightened by the heartbeat that I feel moving rapidly below my finger tips.

My fingers clench his shirt and I pull my chest to his. His hands move to my waist and then lower to the back of my skirt. Neither of us moves for several minutes as we begin making up for lost time.

The magnetic attraction between us is undeniable. Neither of us willing to do what we both want to do, I slowly pull away and rest my hands on his hips. It is such a familiar, yet distant place to be.

I feel him looking at me with the all too familiar eyes that see the caverns of my soul. It seems as if he is deep in thought, but at the same time still very present in the moment.

~

Knowing that I need to quickly spark conversation before the fire between us turns into flames, I prod. Since I was privy to the conversation he just had with an unknown Dr. Turner, I feel entitled to be able to ask some questions.

"So, where are you going for dinner tonight?"

"Oh, we're talking about that now? Okay. Remember when I had to leave to meet a professor at NC State?"

"You mean the day you left so abruptly that I thought you were a ghost?"

"Okay, not very fair. But yes, that's the one. I owe you."

"Don't worry; I'm adding it to the list of IOU's."

"Anyway, it's what I think will be an invitation to teach at NC State."

"I know Anna's thrilled."

"Good try. Keep your day job and don't go into acting."

"I'm hoping we can all have dinner one day together and my kids will babysit for yours." I was well aware he would catch on to my smart-ass tone.

"Hmmph, I guess she would be excited if she knew."

The man who was so confident and cocky ten minutes ago is awkwardly fidgety now.

"So, you're staying in a hotel and your fiancée doesn't know you may be close to not having a long distance relationship?"

"Sam, you won't understand."

"Try me."

"I have been going through life without any physical attachment for a long damn time. I realize it's been lonely at times, but I have found real comfort in making decisions based on what I need and what's best for just me."

"Don't you think that's a bit selfish?"

"Sometimes, but it's a life I've chosen for myself and I haven't hurt anyone by my choices."

"Andy, you have so much to give. You didn't have to make that choice."

Andy shifts his body away from mine and stares out the window for a couple of minutes.

I watch his brows furl and jaw clench. He has always been a deep thinker, hence his love for philosophy. His soul runs deep as he constantly absorbs his own life and those around him. Not easily prodded, I know his angst of whether or not to divulge more of what is in his heart is excruciating to him.

We both see a car pull in front of the boutique and hear two doors shut and realize our time will come to an end soon.

"Sam, I will tell you this. Our time together put an everlasting imprint on my heart. I have never, ever, had a lonely moment because of what we shared."

He leaned over and kissed my forehead and before I knew it, he was gone.

The door opened with the entry of an excited bride and mother and within moments, time was moving again.

Chapter 18

Thank goodness the bride-to-be is perched on cloud nine and doing most of the scouting for her perfect dress because my heart and mind are somewhere else. After two grueling hours which seemed more like twenty, the mother lays down a deposit of one thousand dollars to secure her daughter's dreams.

The gushing bride-to-be takes photos of the gown with her phone to text it to every person she knows. If only a dress could make life so perfect.

While the two had been pulling at seams and fluffing hair around veils, I replayed every moment of my time with Andy. I relive the awkwardness in the parking lot. I visualize his chest pressing against mine and can almost feel the heat that was between us. It wasn't just the heat from the scalding coffee either. Both our bodies boiled and hearts pounded as we made time stand still.

Trying not to run to the door to show them out as soon as their purchase is complete, I sweetly give them a nudge with my Southern charm.

"Oh my, I have to get to my daughter's school for the annual "bring your pet to school day" event. I will be glad to ask my husband to go if you all need some more time."

I offer this option knowing good and well Matt is out-of-town, but feel confident they will be ready to leave.

"No, no, honey. I do not want you to miss such a big event. I remember when Haven had the same rite of passage at her school and look at her now, she's getting married."

"Thank you for your business, and I look so forward to helping to make your day special. I'll be in touch as soon as your gown arrives."

~

What a whirlwind of a day. First, my day began two hours after I went to sleep. Second, I literally have a run in with my old flame that sent sparks flying. Third, Myrtle has no idea what's in store for her in the hands of two dozen second graders. Fourth, it is only noon.

As I enter Stella's classroom I instantly feel calm. My priority at hand is making a room of second graders smile, especially Stella. She instantly sees me and runs over with arms wide open for a quick hug before taking Myrtle in her arms. The little kitten has quickly become a crucial part of our family.

For an hour, Myrtle is passed from arm to arm. Stella beams while she watches her classmates delight in her little fluff ball. Knowing I have a content child, I can leave and feel good with at least this part of my day.

~

I open *je t'aime* for the remainder of the afternoon while trying to keep my mind off the series of morning events. Realizing I have not spoken with Matt in a while, I call to check in.

"Hey! How is it going?"

"Hey, Sam! It's going great. I was just thinking about you and the kids. How did it go taking Myrtle to school?"

"It was the highlight of Stella's day and I have to admit it was mine, too."

"I knew it would be. You're such a good mom."

"At least for the moment, but that could all change by dinner."

"I am actually driving to meet the dean of the Savannah College of Design and I have just arrived at the coffee shop. After, I'm headed straight to the airport and will be home around six."

"We'll be waiting. Love you."

"Love you, too."

Our conversation settles me for the afternoon which allows me to do some desperately needed work. I get excited about the fall couture line and think back to Gran's excitement as she loved the fall and winter gowns. God, I miss Gran. I desperately miss knowing I can call her, rely on her, look to her for guidance.

So deep in thought, I do not even see a car pull up to the door. I hear the chimes at the front door and pause with panic. I will be forever watching the door to see who and what an entrance could bring.

I was absolutely relieved to see Carrie.

"Hey sweetie! I was in the area and knew I had better check on you!"

"Do you have a few minutes?"

"I sure do. I have an hour break until I meet my next client. I assumed no news was good news today. You okay?"

"Yeah, I think so. Hell of a morning. I mean, it wasn't bad, it just *ended* badly."

"What in the world?'

"Andy and I had some pretty intense moments this morning. Physically, we were smoldering. Emotionally, we were reaching into places inside us that have been untouched for years."

"Ok, Sam, you're making me nervous. Go on, please."

"So, we both say some things and ask some tough questions. Questions that definitely got me thinking and ones that made him do the same."

"We instantly picked up where we left off. Carrie, it felt unlike anything else I've experienced in a very long time."

"Sam, did anything happen between you two?"

"No, not like that. But, he did accidentally walk in on me changing."

"Accidentally, Sam?"

"No, really. He went to get us coffee while I was changing from my jogging clothes and he didn't realize I was not dressed."

"Girl, you are so naïve."

"Carrie, all he saw was me without my shirt," I say nonchalantly and wait for her reaction.

"Samantha Lynne! What in the hell were you thinking?"

"It was an utter accident. Besides, if you had stayed, none of this would have happened," I say with a guilty tone.

"I am not on that wax sled to hell with you, my dear," she jokingly says while laughing.

"Ha, ha. Aren't you supposed to by my non-judgmental best friend?"

"No, I'm your conscience. So how did y'all leave things?"

"Of course we were interrupted by an eager bride and her mom so we cut it short. He basically summed it up by saying that the memories from our time together were all he needed in life."

"All he's needed for almost twenty years? Seriously, Sam?"

"The ringer to the situation is that he is here another day to interview for a professorship at NC State."

"Again, holy shit, Sam. So to recap, the man from your past dreams mysteriously shows up and makes you feel like a woman again. He gives you a sappy love story and bam, he leaves?"

"Yeah, that's about it..."

"Sam, did you tell him about the pregnancy and losing the baby. Did you tell him why you disappeared off the earth?"

"Uh, no. No, I didn't, but we didn't have time."

"Sam, don't you think it's eerie how all of this has come up a week after Gran had died? I think it's coming back around for a reason and it's time you deal with all of it."

"It's not time – I don't have time anymore. I have kids and a family that are counting on each moment of my time and this does not fit in."

"Fit in, Sam? Fit in? How can you even say that? You give your heart and soul to your kids and family and you don't *allow* yourself time to have things like this creep in. Have you ever thought about that?" Carrie pauses for a half second before starting again. "Until Gran died, you had not had time alone. No kids, no husband, no Gran. You needed that time and still need it. When you're feeling uncomfortable and wondering what to do next, that is a good thing. You should always be questioning yourself to see if you're being "real." You're one of the strongest people I know for others, but you refuse to go there with yourself."

"How could everything be okay and then bam – this hits me like a ton of bricks?"

"Sweetie, this is not all happening over night; you just woke up."

Wow. My best friend has just pushed me into the Arctic Ocean and told me to swim. After the initial shock, I realize that Carrie is still one of the only people who can tell me what I need to hear and is usually dead-on.

Almost late for a sales call, Carrie realizes she'll have to finish our talk later.

"I'm not done with you and don't you be done with this either. I'm not going to let you sweep it under the carpet, Sam. And by the way, love you, mean it."

Chapter 19

The kids and I spend the rest of what feels like the "Groundhog Day" movie anticipating Matt's return. Stella decides that she will make a sign for him and Graham is going to help me make dinner.

"What should we make tonight?" Graham asks while looking deep into the pantry.

"Very good question. Hmmm, how about we pull open Gran's recipe box and choose?"

Graham is getting so tall that he barely has to reach on his toes for the recipes. He has become a young man literally in the blink of an eye.

"I know we have the makings for her homemade macaroni and cheese, broccoli casserole, seven layer salad, homemade rolls, and peach cobbler."

"That sounds good to me," Graham says while heading to the fridge to begin gathering ingredients.

"Yay, I love mac and cheese!" Stella yells from her room.

Graham and I spend the next hour bonding over making a pretty much guaranteed good feast. Gran's food is fail-proof. I spent hundreds of aroma-filled afternoons with her in the kitchen just as Graham is doing with me now.

When I was a little girl her kitchen was not attached to the main house as was customary for fear of houses burning down due to kitchen fires. We had the kitchen to ourselves since it was away from the main part of the house. We would nibble and taste everything we made. We'd sing old hymns with me as alto and her as soprano. By the time I was a teenager the house and kitchen were enclosed which made the house smell as good as what was in the oven, but we had to be more civilized since Papa was usually close by.

The kitchen was one place Gran really came out of her shell. I think it was part of her emotional therapy as she beat the hell out of chicken tenderizing it or rolling biscuits with all her might. I have no doubt that I equate cooking to a very pleasurable activity in my life because of my time with Gran.

Stella is busily preparing the welcome home sign. I hear her wrestling with Myrtle and Scarlet and her frustration mounts.

"Stella, you okay?" I ask while walking towards her room.

"No, Myrtle and Scarlet are not copperating with me!"

As I walk in I see exactly that she meant to say "cooperating." Stella is holding Myrtle tight in one arm with the other trying to push Myrtle's paw into an ink pad.

"Goodness! What are you doing?"

"I'm trying to put Myrtle and Scarlet in the paint so I can have their paws on the sign."

Stella's creativity and thoughtfulness are precious to me. Bless her heart, she really is trying to make Matt's homecoming special.

"Sweetie, that is such a neat idea. I'm not sure the animals are going to sit still long enough for you to do that, so how about I hold their paws and you trace them?"

"I guess that will work just fine! I've got to trace fast though!"

Stella and I trick the animals long enough to get an image down on the paper. To completely satisfy her design intent, Stella adds some drops of paint to their paw outlines.

"Perfect, mommy! Let's go hang it."

Matt calls when he lands at RDU International which gives us exactly fifteen minutes to tie up loose ends for final "welcome home" preparations.

~

"Daddy's home!"

"Yay, daddy's here!" Graham calls to me as he heads out the front door.

I stand with Scarlet and Myrtle in the door and watch the children tackle their dad before he even makes his way in the door. My soul warms seeing the affection they have for one another. No matter what my path in life could have been, no one else could have created these exact children with me.

The kids literally hang on Matt as he makes his way into the house. Scarlet wags her tail and shows as much energy as her old body can.

"Dinner smells heavenly," Matt says graciously accepting a glass of Riesling.

"I think it will be good because we used Gran's recipe," Graham says as he wipes cheese off the aged handwritten recipe card.

I smile as I am glad to have this little piece of Gran with us tonight. Matt and I recap the highlights of the past few days while the bread completes its final few baking moments.

I decide to focus on the "bring your pet to school day" event so I don't give any clue of my morning strife.

"Myrtle was definitely the hit of the day. I know Stella was proud to have her there."

"Look at her. She's yawning as we speak!"

"She may sleep for days! Enough about my day, it's your turn."

"Actually, I have something to show you," Matt says as he reaches into his large portfolio and lays a canvas on the kitchen island.

"I painted this while you were in Fairfield. I'm going to display it at Cameron Village's Sixtieth Anniversary street festival this weekend."

Holy crap! I completely forgot about the weekend celebration. My mind has been so preoccupied the last few days that I forgot about the anniversary festivities. First thing in the morning, my focus has to change so I can get the boutique prepared. Perhaps this will be a welcomed distraction.

"Honey, it is incredible," I say with earnest as I inspect each and every minute detail.

I am overcome by his expertise in combining the old Cameron Village with the present day look and feel. The older shops and streetscapes merge beautifully with what is now the twenty-first century hustle and bustle. Nestled beautifully at the corner of the cobblestone street is *je t'aime*. Its awning and bench are positioned perfectly and marry the old and new in the most charming manner.

"Matt, I am breathless. You really captured the area with perfection. I am very touched that you highlighted *je t'aime*; the way the light plays on the buildings is spectacular."

"I am so glad you like it and if no one else does, it won't matter at all," he says as he pulls me to his chest.

I don't move for several minutes staying warm and safe in his arms. He knows me and my heart. I know him and his soul. We do things for each other and for our family. For this moment, we're a package. A complete package.

"Mooommmmy, I'm soooo hungry," Stella announces dramatically as she wiggles between us.

"Well, if you can help tickle mommy so she will let go of me, I can help fix the plates of food."

I pretend to be sleeping as I feel Stella's fingers running from my feet up to my under arm. She's quietly whispering "creep mouse" which reminds me of the hundreds of times Gran whispered "creep mouse" to her. Stella starts to tickle my arm and I turn her upside down.

"Mommy, not the *shake!*"

"Daddy, don't you think Stella needs the giggles shaken out of her?" I ask while moving Stella back and forth like a pendulum.

"Without a doubt!"

Graham busts in the kitchen and saves the day for Stella. Grabbing her by the knees, he swoops her away and sets her on the sofa in the living room.

Amazed at his strength and stealth, I am even more surprised at his willingness to help his sister.

"Graham, you saved me! I will give you a dollar from my allowance."

Graham and Stella temporarily unite to have a very peaceful dinner. Graham doesn't even choose something ugly about his sister when I asked him what one funny thing happened during the day.

When it comes around to my turn to recount the daily good, bad and funny, I focus on the fact that I had a large order at the boutique. I decide to focus on my blessings of loving the work I do on a daily basis and the benefit to my family.

Still thankful for the distraction from the morning, we continue our family catch-up time, playing rounds and rounds of war with cards moving as quickly as my emotions from the day.

~

After I finally get the kids get to bed, I am grateful to find Matt fast asleep on the couch. Deciding not to disturb him, I cover his legs and curl up on the opposite end of the sofa.

Again, glad to have some peace and quiet from the roller-coaster day, I catch up on the recorded mind-numbing shows and don't for a moment feel guilty for watching "The Bachelor," "Oprah's Greatest Moments," and "Tori and Dean." Somewhere in the middle of full-blown bickering on "The Bachelor," I fall into a deep sleep. My slumber is abruptly interrupted as Myrtle decides to climb across my chest and face. With one eye still closed, I barely make out the time on the cable box. I know I see a three, which is reason enough to relocate to the bedroom. I gently nudge Matt and lead him to the bedroom for a few more hours of rest.

Chapter 20

The next morning the kids come barreling at top speed to our bedroom. Myrtle peeps her head out of Stella's zipped hoodie as if to say "save me!" Matt pretends as if he is still asleep, grabs Stella and pulls her between the sheets.

"Make me the ham in the sandwich, daddy, pppppllllleeeaaassseee!"

Stella's favorite game is snuggling between the two of us while we wrap our arms around her creating what she calls the "sandwich." Even at eight, she still enjoys the simple little game. I watch Stella and Matt closely. Each of their faces glow with the attention they are showing one another.

Lost in my thoughts, I am startled back to reality with the sound of Matt's cell phone ringing. Still giggling with her daddy, Stella is unaffected by his call. Stella hops on my back and we play mama and baby bear on the way out of the bedroom to give Matt privacy.

With Matt on the phone, I use the time to get the kids ready for school and out the door. He waves and sends a kiss in the air to them before we get in the car for the drive-thru line. Knowing now that I need to focus on the upcoming Cameron Village anniversary weekend, I decide to call Carrie and reschedule our running time.

Eager to find out what transpired during Matt's phone call, I head towards what sounds like singing in the shower.

"Oh, hey.Thanks for taking the kids to school. I was hoping to have relieved you this morning."

"No worries, babe. I could tell it was an important call."

"Yeah, it was. It was actually the dean that I met for coffee before I left yesterday. He's interested in me."

"What do you mean by interested in you?"

"He wants me to teach in Savannah."

Wow, that possibility hit me right out of left field. I was focusing on Andy's potential teaching move, and here's my husband with the possibility of moving and relocating our entire family to another freaking state.

"Well, that's a big deal. I am pretty floored, I must say. How do you feel about it all?"

"The dean, Dave, is a very nice guy. He's built the art program into a solid school over the past decade. They're doing a lot of exciting and progressive projects."

"Is teaching something you're interested in?"

"Well, I haven't really thought about it until now. I would be working with graduate level students and Dave's apparently been following my career for several years."

"You've got a lot to consider."

"No, we have a lot to consider, Sam. I won't make any decisions until we make choices together."

Suddenly, the idea of more decisions makes me feel nauseated. Where has my simple life gone?

"Can we please just move slowly with it all, though?"

Sensing my concern, Matt quickly rebuttals, "Of course, of course. One day at a time."

I repeat Matt's last sentence to myself. It's the same mantra I've been telling myself for the last few days. Maybe I need to slow down even more and go minute by minute...

"How about we get a little breakfast together before I go to *je t'aime*?" I say as I slip off my clothes waiting for my turn in the shower.

"I'm hungry, but I'd love a little taste of you," Matt says as he motions for me to join him in the shower.

It had obviously been a few days since we shared intimate moments. It is definitely rare that we slow down long enough for a morning together without the kids. This lone fact is erotic to me. I am also sensing the need to reconnect with the man I married to help end the daydreams about the man I did not.

Matt slides the shower doors and pulls me in. Years ago I worried about not having a shower *before* making love. Now, I'm just thankful for the privacy without interruption for five minutes.

His body is almost unchanged by time. His soccer toned legs and slight stomach look the same to me now as they did years ago. Never has Matt made me feel self-conscious about my weight and body fluctuations since having babies.

Thankful for the chance to make the shower seat useful, I sit on top of his lap and Matt eases himself into me. I move slowly back and forth feeling him deep inside. He takes my full breasts into his hands and molds them as if he is shaping art. I begin to lose control as I feel my thighs burn hot. As I get close to an eruption, Matt flips me over and brings me home.

For a brief moment, I picture Andy. Quickly, I snap out of my intimate dream to the present and muster up the voice to match the sounds of pleasure coming from Matt. Realizing that I need to be here in this moment both physically and emotionally, I force myself to connect with Matt to help bridge the distance that has begun to build. Not wanting to rush the moment, but knowing the day is waiting, we make our way back again to the shower.

Chapter 21

Knowing another round of caffeine will help jumpstart my day, I stop at the coffee shop to get my morning boost. The local shop owners around *je t'aime* have become almost like family. Over the years, we have all watched storefronts open, close, or grow. Those of us who have made it through the first five years are almost locked arm-in-arm to stick it out together.

After chatting for a few minutes with Barb, the owner and barista, I casually sip my coffee and stroll towards *je t'aime*. As I pass to cross the street to my corner, Jack, the owner of Oberlin Floral Design, runs out the door calling my name.

"Sam, Sam! You're just the person I was heading to see!"

Jack, a handsome man who loved to play with flowers and men, has become a good friend of mine. We have been sending business each other's way for almost a decade. I have become his confidant with boyfriend problems and he has become my constant source of positive energy. In return for relationship help, Jack is always quick to offer his fashion help when I'm skirting fashion failures.

"Hey, Jack. I'm glad you were headed my way. Do you want to get a cup of coffee? I should have brought you one. It'll be my treat!"

"Actually, I am swamped today. Can I have a rain check?"

"Of course!"

"I was about to make a delivery to you."

"Oh my goodness! What's the occasion?"

"Hmmm, I'm not entirely sure. Someone left an envelope in the drop slot this morning with a cash order for you, but there was no name."

Jack disappears into the walk-in cooler and produces a gorgeous arrangement with gardenias, magnolia leaves and purple throated orchids. Gladiolus stems give the heavenly bouquet a pop of color.

"Oh my goodness! Jack, it is gorgeous. You did an incredible job!"

Not even caring who they are from, I cannot get over the scent and magnificence of the arrangement.

"It was easy to make it prettybecause I know you so well, plus the cash went far."

I took a moment to lift the card from its sleeve and almost didn't want to ruin the moment.

"Samantha, congratulations on the success of *je t'aime*. Although it's not your 60th anniversary yet, you and your "boutique" have helped to make Cameron Village what it is today."

As Jack had said, the card is anonymous, but the message speaks loud and clear to me. The reference to "boutique" can certainly point back to Andy, but in my naiveté, I choose not to jump to conclusions.

"Jack, thank you for the gorgeous addition to the festivities this weekend."

"Honey, you deserve them! I'll see you for the celebration!"

As Jack kisses each of my cheeks and hands me my surprise bouquet, I am barely able to manage both the large arrangement and my coffee. What a way to start my day.

~

Maneuvering the flowers and coffee are worth the struggle. The gorgeous arrangement is a perfect centerpiece for the round entrance table. Within minutes, *je t'aime* is filled with the gardenia fragrance. Even though the table and centerpiece are slightly overwhelming for the space, I think they are perfect.

The first time Gran visited the boutique, she brought me a large centerpiece of jasmine, freesia, and hydrangeas. She studied every square inch of the space and began planning additions she thought were necessary. The first on her list was a table for the entrance that would make people feel at home when shopping. At first I thought she was being over the top, but when she added the simple pedestal and glass topper, it warmed the space immediately.

We both envisioned a mix of fun color and elegant formality for a table covering. Gran was eager to shop for fabrics in Raleigh because she "made do" with remnants from small town shops. The timeless fabric we chose was a pastel plaid heavy silk cloth with gold rope cording. We stayed up until two in the morning stitching the final touches. The next morning we spread it across the round table and it was perfect. The edges of the cloth spread softly across the floor creating a tailored look. She had been right – the table provided functionality as well as warmth.

The flowers are a great beginning to the preparation for the anniversary weekend. The sixtieth anniversary will draw thousands of visitors to the cobblestone streets of Cameron Village. I want to attract former customers as well as future ones. Many storefronts will be having sidewalk sales to lure guests. I have to be creative with *je t'aime*'s presence since the nature of my business is pretty unique for the shopping area.

Thankful for the continued distraction, I continue to plan out the day. I decide that a fashion show with flower girl, ring bearer, bridesmaid and wedding gown fashions will draw people of all ages. I design a flyer to be included at the morning kickoff activities and begin calling my troops to flaunt their stuff.

Kate, our babysitter from NC State, enlists several "sisters" from her sorority, ZTA, to be bridesmaids and brides for the day. I count Graham and Stella as two of the young models and call a few of their friends to walk the carpet as young members of the wedding party. Last but not least, I coerce Carrie to put on a wedding gown and join the fun.

"Sam, I will do it as long as you do, too!"

"Sure, why the hell not, right? It will be fun!"

The remainder of the afternoon flies by as I pull the gowns and tuxedos to steam out the wrinkles. The walkway will be a blush colored velvet that I used for a TV advertisement. It is a perfect width of three feet and the final touch with include a scattering of hot pink rose petals. I call Jack to order five hundred petals which he graciously gives to me if I promise to let him help set up the show.

The night sails smoothly with our "Groundhog Day" routine of the good, bad, and not-so-good parts of the day. Liking the routine with Matt back and the comfortable predictability of our days, I have almost forgotten about Andy. Maybe the flowers were from him as a "good job, kid" kind of sentiment. None the less, I feel proud of *je t'aime* and am thrilled to be a part of the special commemorative day tomorrow.

Chapter 22

The morning begins with its normal hustle and bustle plus the additional excitement of the festivities. Matt packs the car with his paintings to display along the sidewalk in front of Seagrove Pottery and I pack hairspray, makeup and other odds and ends needed for the fashion show.

When we arrive, the kids help me place plastic pastel tubs with ice and beverages in strategic places around the boutique. Graham suggests adding a tub on a stand outside the door to help lure visitors inside. Stella and I place the butter mints, cucumber sandwiches and cheese straws on crystal plates and doilies on a sidebar table. This menu would make Gran proud for sure.

Carrie arrives with one hand ready for a hug and the other holding a bottle of champagne.

"Sam, Graham, and Stella, *je t'aime* is gorgeous! You all have made it extra special today!"

"I couldn't have done it without my little helpers."

"I thought we could toast the occasion. Where's Matt?"

"He's setting up around the corner in front of Seagrove. I'd actually love for you to see his tribute to the anniversary. Let's all walk over and check out what daddy's doing."

"Sounds great!"

It's a beautiful spring morning with perfect weather for the celebration. Stores are busily attaching balloons and other novelties to their unique spaces. Each of the stores has character which is what makes Cameron Village so special. Perhaps it's the nostalgic setting that makes me feel peaceful in my busy life. It's the one piece of my world that's somewhat controllable.

Matt's on his way to meet us when we see him leaving Seagrove.

"Hey guys!"

"How's it going setting up? I wanted Carrie and the kids to see your art, especially the anniversary piece."

"Absolutely. They're right in here."

Seagrove Pottery is a perfect place to highlight his artistry even though he does not have pottery. With its local focus, Seagrove has featured regional artists for decades and for the anniversary, they invited Matt to showcase and display his art. Matt's work is hung on a vertical wall board with spotlights positioned perfectly on each of them. His "anniversary" piece as I call it is simply perfect. Your eye is immediately drawn to the spectacular work.

"Daddy, I love this one that shows mommy's store. Can we have it and not sell it?"

"I'm glad you like it, Graham. I think it's a great idea to have one in mommy's store. This one goes up for auction today, but I'll paint her a new one."

"Daddy, what's an auction?"

"This afternoon, people are going to name a price for artwork and other items. Whoever says the highest price gets to take the item home. The money earned will go towards funding other downtown renovation projects. Actually, maybe we can all go and you guys can see how it works. What time is the fashion show again?"

"It's at two this afternoon and I need you there," I say as I put my arm around his waist.

"You know I won't miss it. The auction is one of the last events of the festivities and starts at five so I think we'll be okay."

"I may try and win your mommy's painting," Carrie says as she winks at the kids.

"Goodie gumdrops," Stella says while jumping up and down.

"Let's go toast to today with champagne Carrie brought."

"Hell, yes," Matt says with pride.

~

When we get back to *je t'aime*, we complete the final details of the day. Jack joins us temporarily between floral orders to add a few special touches. He's lit two dozen gardenia votives and added a floating candle and gardenia centerpiece to the refreshment area.

"Oh Jack, now it's perfect!"

"Not yet, my dear," he says while reaching for my shirt to attach a corsage.

"Now it is," Jack says as he does his French "moi, moi" kiss in the air.

"Jack, we've come a long way, baby."

"Speak for yourself, honey. I hope to never grow up!" Jack says as he waves and scurries back to the land of flowers.

"Wow, I wish I had a Jack in my life," Carrie muses.

"He's something, all right! He has that unique eye for detail that just makes things special."

"He's also a perfect male best friend to have because Matt has no worries about the time I spend with him."

"He's probably trying to spend time with you to get to Matt!"

"Can't say that's not true!"

Guests begin to arrive. Some browse for gowns while others enjoy looking around and retelling stories of what used to stand in *je t'aime's* location sixty years ago. Carrie helps to write up four large orders while Stella and Graham serve refreshments to anyone who looks their way.

"You must be Samatha," says a white haired woman dressed in a gorgeous periwinkle suit.

"Yes, ma'am," I say offering my hand.

"You don't know me but I knew your grandmother, Ada Grace, very well. My name is Ruth Minges."

My heart skipped a beat. I haven't heard Gran called "Ada Grace" since her funeral. This woman was dressed elegantly – just as Gran would have looked. Women of her era never left the house without looking "proper" and "respectable."

"Oh, wow, nice to meet you Mrs. Minges. Gran mentioned you many times. Weren't you two roommates at East Carolina's Teaching College?"

"First of all, call me Ruth, please," she says in her Blanche DuBuois accent.

"That is correct. Ada Grace and I shared a room for almost a year before I had to leave school. We had a good old time."

"Why did you leave?"

"It was the year the Depression hit and my family lost everything they had. My parents did everything they could to keep me there, but they needed me to earn money."

"Oh, Ruth, I am so sorry."

"Sweetie, it is just fine. We ended up moving to Raleigh to live with family and it's here that I met the love of my life. Actually, we walked through these same streets hand in hand many years ago. Of course, everything looked much different then."

"Well I'm certainly glad things worked out for you. Is your husband still alive?"

"No, dear, I actually lost him to a fight with Alzheimer's the same week Ada Grace died. I wanted so badly to see her before she passed away, but I couldn't leave my husband, Tommy. She had called once when she got settled with you and your family in Raleigh and we enjoyed catching up. It was so good to hear her voice."

"I am so sorry about your husband, Tommy."

"Dear, I am sorry about your losing Gran, too. She was such a special woman who loved you and your little family dearly."

"How did you know where to find me?"

"She told me all about your place here and went on and on about it."

"I had no idea she had called you. I would have taken her to see you in her final months."

"She told me she was too weak to get out and about the city so I didn't push her. We visited by phone and that was almost as special. Seeing you here now makes me feel as if I've had a vision of her."

"Wow, I really appreciate your sharing this with me," I say fighting back tears and reaching for a hug.

"Samantha, the pleasure is all mine. I would love to stop by occasionally if you don't mind."

"I would love it. Anytime at all. We're having a fashion show at two this afternoon if you'd like to come back and see my kids all dressed up."

"Well, I just might come. I am having lunch with some friends and then we might all come back by."

My morning is made by this priceless interaction. I am eager for any memories of Gran that will help keep her memory alive. She wouldn't have missed this day for the world. As I look around the bustling boutique watching goodies being enjoyed and the many charming touches that she recommended, I realize Gran is all around.

~

Jack reappears like clockwork to help the "models" look snazzy for the show.

"Sam, you owe me big time for pulling me away from the shop," Jack says in a breathless voice.

"Oh, Jack, I am so sorry. Are you slammed with business today? It was very thoughtless for me to assume you would be able to help me today. This is your day at the floral shop, too." Guilt sets in and settles with a nice shade of pink on my cheeks.

"No, Sam, it's fine. We have had one order all day. I haven't had a chance to tell you that I hired a manager to fill in when I can't be there."

"Jack, that's great! It's about time. You need a break every now and then!"

"That's the problem. My new hire is super-duper cute and I

don't want to take vacation now because I want to be able to see his cute ass in jeans!"

"Shhh, here come the kids. Keep your romantic fantasies in your head for the next hour, please!" I say while punching his arm.

Stella's three friends can barely contain their excitement to try on flower girl and junior bridesmaid attire. Graham's buddies look appropriately distraught, but I can tell the four ten year-old boys are somewhat proud.

With the pink runner and petals perfectly placed, it is the perfect setting for the show. Matt places white wood chairs on either side of the pseudo runway while Carrie and I go behind the scenes to get everyone dressed. Jack does the initial hair and makeup touch-ups and then I send him out front to be the emcee for the event.

It's two minutes before show time and I peep between the crack of the storage room curtains. My mind flashes back to the last time I looked between the same crack and saw Andy looking no different than he did almost two decades ago.

Today, people known and unknown are supporting *je t'aime* in what looks to be standing room only. Front and center are Ruth and four of her white-haired friends. They sit sedately with their perfectly placed hair and red lipstick anticipating the event.

Jack notices my feeble attempt to hide my eyes from the guests and winks at me. He looks as proud as I do. Over the years, we have watched our businesses grow and thrive. Much like his floral design business, some years at *je t'aime* are better than others. We've stuck with the good and bad to be able to relish times like these.

Carrie gets the models lined up while Jack begins the show. He is right at home front and center with a microphone in his hand.

"Thank you, ladies and gentlemen for joining us at *je t'aime* today for our spring formal extravaganza. You will see the latest in fine couture fashion, but *je t'aime* has access to many more beautiful designs than we have time to show today. After the show, please pick up a catalog featuring more about *je t'aime* and the collections represented. Now, let's get this show going!"

Matt starts the iPod and the first song, "Glamorous," begins the processional of the bridesmaid gowns. Gorgeous college girls strut their stuff on the pink aisle highlighting gorgeous hues of purple, pink, green, blue, and black. Jack never skips a beat perfectly describing each young lady and gown.

While the girls have a quick outfit change, Jack uses the time to give a quick history of *je t'aime*.

"The owner of this exquisite boutique is the lovely Samantha. She and her family are longtime Raleigh residents. Look closely and you will see her son and daughter later in the show. Now, I present to you gowns that will make your heart melt!"

Matt cues up the iPod again, but this time with the music of Jason Mraz's, "I'm Yours." The ZTA girls twirl and float once again down the petal lined runway. The next song cued is "Love Story" by Taylor Swift, which is perfect for the introduction of the flower girls and ten year-old fellas in their handsome tuxedos. This part steals the show as the young wedding models soften the hearts of everyone in the room.

Graham and Stella make one more outfit change. Carrie and I slip into the gowns we chose that will hopefully be perfectly beautiful, acceptable, and sexy for thirty-something brides. Graham and Stella escort Carrie and me down the aisle for the last showing. Matt fades Taylor Swift into Top Gun's "Take My Breath Away."

Graham looks at us and mouths, "What *is* this song?"

Carrie and I both smile as I search the crowd for Matt so I can give him a "thank you" wink.

As I scan the room I see a tall gentleman near the front door. I do a double-take and my heart stops – Andy is leaning confidently on the wall watching my every move. To his right is his seemingly underage fiancée and two of her platinum blonde BFF's.

My legs feel like they weigh five hundred pounds. I'm suddenly stunned and Carrie notices the immediate change. While Stella and Graham make their walk down the runway, she gives me the "eye" desperately trying to figure out what is going on. I give a nod towards the front door and she immediately recognizes the pink elephants in the room – the athletic, unmarried, old beau standing by the door with his whiny bride-to-be.

My initial reaction is to run as fast as I can to flee the room that is quickly closing in around me, but HE is standing at my exit. Dammit, I have got to keep it together. This day and moment are way too important to me and my family.

Thank goodness for Jack nearly yelling in the microphone to jolt me from my stupor. "Now, I would like to introduce to you the lovely owner and creator of *je t'aime*, Sam."

Jack passes the microphone to me with the biggest smile on his face. If he only knew what my inner dialogue was saying, he would die!

"First of all, I would like to thank each and every one of you for taking the time to join us today for this special anniversary. *je t'aime* is a part of my family and I am proud and thankful that I've been able to share it with the community for almost fifteen years. If I could have my models join me out front, I can give proper thanks."

While I wait for the eight, ten, and twenty-something's to join me on the pink runway, I finally see Matt by the front counter and feel instant relief. He looks so damn proud of us, of this moment.

Carrie walks Stella and Graham over to me and I take their hands.

"My next set of thanks goes out to everyone who has made this day special. To all of these gorgeous models, let's give them a round of applause."

The college girls each take a hand of the younger kids which makes the little ones light up with pride.

"To Jack, our emcee, organizer and relentless friend, you never cease to amaze me." We complete the thanks with an appropriate air hug and kiss.

"This young lady, my right arm for more than thirty-five years, has supported me from day one of the inception of *je t'aime*. She never once told me, or at least so I could hear, that I was crazy. I appreciate her support more than anyone will ever know."

As I hug her, my position angle has me looking straight into Andy's eyes. Our gaze locks as if he can own much of the gratitude and in part, he can. Knowing I can't leave anyone out in my gratitude speech, I break my stance with Carrie and Andy's stare to keep acknowledging folks.

"Last but not least, my family, Matt, Stella and Graham, live *je t'aime* with me each and every day. Their support and love give me the energy that I need to help believe in what I do. I couldn't be more appreciative of my little family."

Matt hands the kids a bouquet of wildflowers hand-tied with a ribbon to present to me and when they do, the tears begin to flow. The flowers remind me of Gran and I appreciate Matt's special touch to the day.

"Some of you may or may not know this, but we lost a very dear woman close to our hearts not so long ago. My graceful, smart, witty grandmother blessed the world with her presence for almost one hundred years. She, too, was a part of creating *je t'aime* and I feel her presence each day. She paved the way for me to be a woman with endless dreams and drive. For that I will be forever...grateful."

Carrie walks over and rests her arm around my waist and her head on my shoulder.

Mustering up the voice to wrap up the final moments of the show, I scan the audience being sure to make eye contact with everyone. Even Andy. "Well, I think we've had a truly wonderful afternoon enjoying beautiful people and fashion! Again, how about another round of applause for *je t'aime* and the models."

Everyone stood up and cheered for us one last time. Ruth blew me a kiss with her Southern graceful moves and Andy looked at me as if he had never left twenty years earlier.

Chapter 23

After the show, I meet dozens of new people and reestablish contact with past patrons. My heart is overjoyed while I use this opportunity to soak up the positive energy. Matt comes to my side and gently squeezes my arm.

"Excuse me, ladies, one second. I need to borrow my wife."

"Honey, I am so proud of you. It all went off without a hitch. You three looked beautiful and elegant."

"Thank you. I think it did, too. The flowers overwhelmed me. Thank you."

"Well, they're not as spectacular as the ones on the round table, but maybe they'll do." Matt glances at the overpowering bouquet that is screaming "here I am."

I guess this confirms they are not from him.

"Oh my goodness. The wildflowers are absolutely perfect and mighty in impact."

"I hate to do this, but I need to get back to Seagrove. I'll see you guys at five?"

"Absolutely. You wanna take the kiddos with you so they can have a change of scenery?"

"Sure, that's a good idea. There's face painting and crafts right outside the pottery. See you soon."

"Love you, guys. See you in a couple of hours." I call and turn back towards my guests, but not before my attention immediately shifts outside to the beverage tub. All I see are Matt and Andy exchanging words and I literally leap towards the door. Carrie immediately understands the urgency and takes my place with the two men. After a minute, she and Andy make their way towards me. The last of my guest "models" leave and the crowds begin to thin.

"What in the hell was that?" I say to Andy in an accusatory tone.

"Sam, relax. Don't give Andy the Spanish inquisition," Carrie says in a hushed tone.

"Matt does NOT know who you are and I hope you kept it

that way." Realizing my voice is getting louder and tenser, I turn my back to both Andy and Carrie.

"Sam, relax. He and I were reaching for a drink at the same time so I offered to get him one," Andy says as he reaches for my arm.

"Seriously, Sam, that was it. Let's move on from this. Plus, we need to get out of these gowns before someone thinks we're runaway brides!" Carrie says to try and smooth the scene.

"Fine. Let's take turns changing so we don't leave the showroom unattended."

"Good idea!" Carrie says with relief in her eyes.

"Definitely a good idea to have someone here with us when you're changing," Andy says in a cocky tone.

Not needing to go down that road at this moment, I reach for a strand of hair to tuck and realize it's pulled up for the fashion show. Andy pulls a few strands loose and tenderly tucks them behind my ear. Not having words for the occasion, I look up into his beautiful eyes and just smile.

"Sam, your kids are just like you. I know you're proud."

"Thanks. I can't take all the credit, but I think they're pretty awesome, too. By the way, where's your fiancée and her entourage?"

"Not sure. I think they went for a manicure or something. Who knows? Anyway, I hope you feel great about the day."

"Definitely. I think it came together pretty well in just two days."

"Damn, you were always the one to push the envelope."

"I guess I still am."

A bride and her mother approach us with what looks like a notebook of ideas and questions. As always, this is going to be a meeting cut short.

"Sam, great job. Gran would have been so proud."

I watch him leave yet again, but today he is not in a rush. He is more calculated in his exit almost as if he knows I am watching.

"Glad you got the flowers..."

My face blushes the color of the pink runway. Within seconds he disappears into the masses of people walking the streets of Cameron Village.

The eager bride and her mother produce multiple examples of magazine styles and within an hour, I have her in a gown, deposit paid, and bridesmaid appointments set. Carrie finishes writing up the details while I change out of the gown. I've now worn this gown longer than I wore my own.

I check my cell phone voicemail and see that I have a text message. It's a video from Andy. I play it and quickly turn down the blaring volume. It's three minutes of me doing my "thank you" speech. Wow, that's me in the wedding gown with my two beautiful children at my side. I replay it twice and watch my face looking full of content and joy. I look like a strong and confident woman. Gosh, I look all grown-up and actually feel the way I looked in the video.

Extremely appreciative to Andy for taking the time to video and share it with me, I text

"thx for this. It's priceless…"

I assume Anna and her friends were too caught up with each other to notice the filming. Just as I put my phone away, Carrie walks in to unzip me.

"Whew, the last customer just left and I locked the door. What an amazing day!"

"I totally agree. Thank you so much. I truly couldn't have done it without you."

"It was fun dressing up. It felt like we were eight again trying on fancy clothes. Besides, I wouldn't have missed this drama for a million dollars!"

"Damn, did he really have to show up today?

"I almost fainted, so I know you must have been dying inside."

"You have no idea."

"Sweetie, I think I do. I see the way he looks at you. Andy watches you without your even knowing."

"I know, right? I didn't feel panicky today when he left. I'm thinking it was because he was almost a part of the family today. Weird, very weird, I know."

"I, honest to God, do not think he would ever intentionally hurt you or your family. It's almost as if y'all have a bond that is impenetrable. I can feel it between you two."

I pause as I slip on my final pieces of clothing. I know exactly what she means. It's an unspoken energy between us that I don't know how to "file away" and feel sure he doesn't either.

Sensing my internal struggle, Carrie is quick to ease my mind.

"Hon, you can't solve it today and maybe not even tomorrow. Don't feel overwhelmed."

"Shit. It's kinda hard not to feel overwhelmed. I do know that I need to wrap my head around all of this. Long ago I tried to rewrite our history and hide pieces that I didn't want him to know. I've got to figure this out and soon." I say in my matter-of-fact all business tone.

Knowing she wasn't going to get a last word, Carrie salutes me and says, "Yes, ma'am."

Chapter 24

Carrie and I gather with Matt, the kids and Jack for the auction. I easily count hundreds of people who have come out to support the fundraiser benefitting 'Raleigh's Downtown Renovation initiative. We're gathered at one of my favorite places in the village – the library. As I look around the large space, I can remember the times Gran and I browsed the bookshelves for hours and the countless days the kids and I have spent in the middle of the floor reading *Curious George* books.

With at least two hundred people in attendance, it is standing room only for the auction festivities. The kids have their eyes on many items from art, jewelry, vacation packages, dinner certificates, designer shoes to a hand painted artist rendering for any room in the house.

"I've got my eye on the vacation packages," Jack says as he balances his checkbook on his pointer finger.

"Oh, you don't have to take me!" Carrie says in a playful tone over his shoulder.

"You'd be my *second* choice, honey," he says as he winks at Matt.

"Jack, you've got a deal," Matt says as he punches Jack's arm.

"You're cute, Matt, but you're taken!"

The bidding begins and the kids watch with wide eyes. The items go for inflated prices mainly for the good cause, but also for the sake of appearances. The auctioneer announces Matt's art items next and our pseudo-groupie entourage waits and watch. Stella crosses her fingers.

"Please get it, Aunt Carrie, please get it."

The bidding begins at fifty dollars and within seconds it is well over three hundred dollars. Carrie is right in the game until a voice from the back of the crowd calmly calls out "one thousand dollars." The crowd pauses for a moment to look at the big spender.

Towering over the crowd is none other than Andy. Oh shit. Not again. Carrie looks at me with her mouth wide open and one eyebrow raised.

"Don't worry, honey, I'm sure he'll give it to you anyway," Carrie whispers in a sarcastic tone.

"Sold to the gentleman in the back for one thousand dollars."

"Fudgsicles," Stella laments.

That's much nicer than I am thinking. Why in the hell does he have to continue mixing with my family and why now?

"Wow, Sam! Did you hear that?"

"Yep, I sure did."

"I am going to meet that guy. I want to shake his hand. You wanna come with me?"

With nausea erupting in my throat I mutter, "Oh, honey, I think it would be more meaningful coming from just you. He may be a little shy and want anonymity from too many people."

"Good point. I'll be back in a few." Almost skipping with excitement, Matt leaves to have his second meeting with the man I used to love.

Carrie watches them closely and gets within earshot of the conversation. Knowing her face very well, I can tell all is cool.

Not feeling fully comfortable enough to leave the scene, I decide to send the kids over to the "boys." Hopefully they will be a distraction and end this seemingly cheerful meeting. I carefully watch and, thank God, the lovefest ends almost instantaneously and I immediately bolt for home.

Chapter 25

The night is a welcome end to a wonderful but taxing day. Matt comes home on cloud nine as his art pieces produce nearly three thousand dollars for the community.

"Here you go, thought you might like this," I say as I hand him a glass of his favorite wine.

"Thanks and I do want it. Stella fell asleep in the car so let me carry her to the bedroom first."

"I'll get Graham tucked in, too."

After the kids are sleeping like rocks, we sit down and enjoy a glass of Riesling together on the back porch. Scarlet curls up by my feet and Myrtle slumbers on Matt's lap.

"You know, you've never had an allergy to Myrtle have you?"

"No, I haven't which is weird. I'm very glad though because I did not want to give her up."

We enjoy the quiet night both reflecting on the day. I could not have been prouder of *je t'aime* or my family. Matt had a rewarding day from the fruits of his labor, too.

"I heard from one of the organizers that around two thousand people came out to the celebration today. Do you have any idea how many visitors you had at *je t'aime*?"

"Not nearly that many. However, Graham had a counter and he supposedly clicked nearly four hundred times. Not bad for a days' work!"

"Seagrove asked me to duplicate the paintings that sold today since they did so well. I think I may do that over the next few weeks."

"That's a great idea, Matt. You should be so proud."

"Thanks and actually, I am. I still can't believe the "anniversary" painting went for one thousand dollars. The fella said he is relocating to NC State as a professor in the summer. Seemed like a nice guy who must be emotionally invested in the Cameron Village downtown area."

"Hmmm, that's pretty neat." Emotionally invested, that's an understatement.

Desperately trying to change the subject, I focus on a topic I know will consume him.

"Speaking of professorship, have you given your offer any more thought?

"Actually, I have. I don't want to change our life so drastically that we have to start all of this anew. You have worked so damned hard at establishing *je t'aime* and our lives here in Raleigh. I don't want to sacrifice all of this for one job."

"I know what you're saying, but this is not just a job opportunity. This is a profession change that could be a lifetime chance for you. What if we were able to do both? You could teach in Savannah and I could open a second boutique there. We could almost live between cities. You know?"

"I haven't thought about that possibility until you just said it. How could we afford to do that and where would the kids go to school?"

"I haven't quite figured all of that out yet. The money part may be okay once Gran's estate is settled. I'm not sure about the schooling. I guess this is where we need to take baby steps, right?"

"Yep, but I'm liking that we have possibilities. Before I can think clearly, I have to get some rest."

Possibilities - that is an interesting word and one that is actually paralyzing to me at the moment.

"Me, too, but I'm not quite ready to go inside. It's been a wonderful, but long day. I'll be in a few minutes."

"Love you."

"Love you, too."

Scarlet lifts her head to see Matt's movement then easily settles back to sleep on the deck. Matt hands Myrtle to me while I rock in Gran's old wicker chair until I doze off under the starry sky.

Chapter 26

"What time did you come to bed last night?" Matt says as his kisses my ear and hands me our morning caffeine.

"I felt Scarlet nudge me to come inside and I think it was around two. It was getting a little nippy."

"It was cold in the bed without you, too," he says pulling me close to his chest.

"We had a good day yesterday, didn't we?"

"Yes we did. We've made a good life here, Sam. I don't want to throw it away haphazardly."

"Me either. Baby steps."

We lay under the covers silent for several minutes before Matt's phone jars us from deep thought.

"It's the dean again. I'll just be a minute."

Closing the bedroom door behind me to give him a few minutes of privacy, I use the time check email and see what's on our agenda for the day. Ah – birthday gifts and transportation. Besides that, I think it will be a quiet day.

Noticing that June is quickly approaching, I am suddenly reminded that I need to honor Gran's last request which is to plant wildflowers under the elm tree at the lodge. With everything going on, I draw a yellow flower around the date to make sure I don't fail to complete this task.

Matt joins me in the breakfast room and waits for me to finish an email on my BlackBerry. We are both trying to make a real effort not to have our laptops and phones out when we're talking. As soon as I press send, I put it away.

"Sam, they really want me there for the first summer session. I know we haven't made our decision yet, but Dean Miller has invited us to come down as soon as we have a chance. He wants the kids to come, too. What do you think?"

"Don't you think if we take the kids we're much more invested? Maybe we should go first and then take the kids later if we are seriously considering it."

Matt thinks for a minute and takes my hand in his. "Thank you, Sam, for being willing to go with me. It means a lot."

"I know it does. Maybe it'll be good for us to get away for a bit."

Time with just the two of us can only be good. We spend the next few minutes looking at our calendars and decide that with June on its way, we better go towards the end of the week.

I somewhat reluctantly begin lining up the Georgia trip. Not necessarily because I don't want to go, but because I am simply exhausted both physically and emotionally. Knowing that I need to be a supportive partner, I call Kate, our favorite sitter other than Carrie, and get her lined up.

"Sam, you know I'd love to do it. I can't wait. I might even take the kids to a lacrosse game at State next Saturday morning. Oh, by the way, my friends loved modeling yesterday. We had a blast!"

Kate is one of the peppiest people I've ever known, which is why the kids love her. I wish I could get away with saying things like "blast" and "sweet," but it's just not possible anymore. Nonetheless, she is one of the people I feel comfortable keeping the kids.

I know Carrie would be more than willing to stay with the kids, but I try hard to reserve her for running the store, which gives me great comfort as well. With Kate lined up, I call and chat with Carrie as I make my way to Barnes and Noble to buy birthday presents. We talk about Matt's job opportunity and the pros and cons for the family.

"Are you available to watch *je t'aime* on Saturday?"

"I am until about five, but then I'll need to close up to get ready for a..."

I listen and wait for her to finish her sentence.

"Carrie, are you trying to say date?"

"Yes. A date. A d-a-t-e. I can't believe I said it out loud!"

"You're going to make me use OMG! Who is he? How did you meet him?"

"Crazy to say but I've actually known him for a while. He was an intern with me years ago at the radio station and I ran into him again at the gym. We became friends on Facebook and we've been keeping in touch. No big deal, just a good friend."

"God, I have got to get on Facebook so I can check him out."

"I've been telling you the same thing for years, my dear."

"Moving on because you can't teach an old dog new tricks! Carrie, that's awesome! Is he cute?"

"He is actually very cute; cuter than he used to be or maybe my standards have changed," Carrie muses.

"I'm so excited for you and can't wait to hear about it! Keep me posted."

"You know I will! Love ya, mean it."

After we hang up, a smile extends from head to toe for my best friend. The moment of her feeling comfortable enough to get out and date has been long in coming. Maybe her heart is finally healing and opening up again.

Chapter 27

The beginning of the week is slammed for me as I try to get prepared for Savannah. Matt buzzes around town and the house on cloud nine. He can barely wait to head south. Monday and Tuesday are consumed with finishing orders for the mass of summer weddings. With eight new orders from the anniversary festivities, I do not want them to slip behind all that is going on outside of *je t'aime*.

Wednesday is interspersed with business and details of the weekend. In my control-freak fashion, I leave detailed notes for Carrie and type out an insanely detailed itinerary for the babysitter. Thinking of every potential emergency, I leave an emergency contact list for each possible scenario. I put Carrie as the next-in-line contact, but hesitate in hopes she will be completely consumed by her date.

Realizing a cup of coffee will rescue me from the monotonous details, I stroll to my favorite coffee shop and enjoy the change of scenery. Only gone fifteen minutes, I miss a package delivery at the door. It's a large wrapped brown package leaning against the bench. I guess the deliverer felt okay with my "Be Back in 15 Minutes" sign to leave it.

I amuse myself with the precarious coffee juggling situations I get in. It seems as if I'm always trying to carry too much, but damned and determined not to put down something to ease my struggles! The large package fits perfectly on the chaise. I carefully unwrap it and as a corner is revealed, I see a familiar sight. It's the frame of the anniversary painting. Shit. Damn. Not again.

I sit dumbfounded on the chaise for several minutes when once again, I am startled by the door. Certain Andy has made his appearance, I am started by Matt's presence.

"Oh, hey! What are you doing? Everything okay?"

"Don't seem so shocked. I was in the neighborhood and wanted to see my beautiful wife."

"Well, thank you. I was just finishing up a few things for the weekend."

"Me, too. I stopped by Clark Art to borrow several works that

I want to take to Savannah this weekend."

Matt's face makes a quick change as he walks towards the chaise. Knowing exactly what he's seeing, I wait for the question.

"Whoa, Sam, why is my painting here?"

"I walked to get a cup of coffee and when I came back, it was propped up against the bench. There was no note, so I'm assuming the gentleman who purchased it wanted it to be enjoyed."

I feel somewhat vindicated with this explanation because it is not untrue. Not that it is all fact either, but I think speculation is just fine in this situation.

"Oh, wow. Well, what a surprise. It will look perfect in here and I guess when I told him the story of why I did the particular perspective, he remembered the details."

"I'm glad you told him all of that so it could make its way back to me."

"Actually, this is perfect. I'll take it with us this weekend to Savannah!"

In my wildest dreams I never imagined this moment would include the word perfect.

"Do you want to take it now so we don't forget to pack it?" I desperately try to keep the situational momentum going.

"If you don't mind; I think that is a great idea."

Matt heads out, has the painting in his car within seconds and is now on his way to riding the top of cloud nine.

With another tenuous situation narrowly avoided, I try to decide whether I need to thank Andy personally. Of course I should. He spent one thousand dollars for me to have the painting my husband created. How crazy. Maybe he's just trying to be a friend who lost touch and is making up for lost time.

I watch the minute hand on the clock the last three hours of the day. To help my mood I pop Dave Matthews in the CD player and crank it up as loud as possible without becoming too noticeable to customers. After three internet orders and two FedEx deliveries, I decide to call it a day. Before I go home, however, I feel like a run will do me good.

I head to the storeroom to turn off the lights and change into my running clothes. As I pull my hair into a ponytail I hear the door shut. I am so ready to let some tension out and do not feel like attending to another bride today.

"I see you got the package from the front door," Andy says as he walks towards me.

"When are you going to stop doing that?" I joke.

"You mean giving you packages or showing up?"

"Okay, both of them," I say as I tuck a few stray hair pieces behind my ears.

Feeling awkward with the timing, I walk over and give him a hug as if he is an old pal. I slap his back twice and try to pull away.

"What's gotten in to you – are you scared of me now?"

"Scared of you, yeah right," I say as he pulls me towards him with a jolt, trying to be tough. The impact was electric – it was hard, but soft. I stood there frozen in his lock. There it is again - the passion and the heat. I feel his back with its strong muscles and begin thinking that my body must not feel nearly the same as it did fifteen years ago before two children.

Knowing what is ahead of me this weekend and the events of the past one, I tense up and begin to pull away.

"Sam, I can tell something is going on. What is it?"

"Look, I'm fine. I can't tell you what's in my heart because we can't be those people; the kind of people who need each other to figure life out."

Not letting me get away with just that, Andy just stares at me waiting for more.

"You know - two people who share their hearts, hopes and dreams."

"Ah, here it is. You're freaked out because I'm back. You're not sure what to do with me."

Andy pulls away, too, and crosses his arms.

"I hear you, Sam, but doesn't this feel good? Haven't you missed being able to talk and share?"

"Andy, do you realize that Matt doesn't know anything about you? Nothing. Nada. Zip. Do you know why that is? I've had to do a lot of soul searching about you and about this situation."

"Situation? Situation, Sam? It makes it sound like we're freaking business partners."

"It is a situation to me because this is new to me again and I was not prepared to deal with it. I sure as hell wasn't prepared to deal with you," I say as my volume elevates.

"Well, as easily as this messy situation came into your life, it can leave."

As Andy walks towards the door, I run past him and lock the door.

"You're not going anywhere, buddy. You have wanted to talk to me for years and now that you can, you're ready to run out at the slightest bit of frustration?"

With my tough as nails attitude, I go window by window shutting the curtains for the day.

"Sam, you just told me you are not ready for me, for this. What the hell do you expect me to do?"

"Andy, what do you want from me? Do you want us to be best friends? Do you want me to order you wedding clothes for a marriage you and I both know shouldn't happen? Do you want me to pretend you are a long lost acquaintance that I haven't thought about in fifteen years? What, what do you want?"

Andy takes my shoulders and spins me around. Leaning me against the cash register table, he takes my cheeks in his hands and plants his strong lips against mine. It was a hard kiss, forceful with intent.

I quickly pull away and look up into his eyes. I know I should feel miserable with myself for the kiss, but instead, I put my hand through his thick hair and pull his head down to mine again. My knees weaken as we share the most passionate kiss I have ever had in my life.

Andy lifts me up to the table where we are eye to eye.

"Sam, this is what I want. You are what I want. However I can have you is okay. I have to have you in my life."

"Damn, Andy, this feels so good. You feel so good. I can't even tell you what this is doing to me. I haven't felt this in years – or since you left."

Not able to take any more, I bow my head in my hands and start to cry. Andy takes my cheek in his hand and I rest there for several minutes.

"Sam, I know this is confusing. It's a lot to process and I know that. I also know that you have it in you to be able to deal with all of your feelings, whatever they may be. Whoever or whatever you need to move through all this, please find it because I can't handle you brushing me under the carpet again."

Andy hops up to the table and sits beside me hand in hand. After several minutes he breaks the silence. "Where are you going to hang the painting?"

Shit. Here it all is again. If only Andy will think the answer he's about to hear is "perfect."

I whisper softly, "Matt and I are taking it to Savannah this weekend. But I promise it will be hanging next week."

Andy lets go of my hand. "Savannah? Why?"

"Matt was offered a teaching position in Savannah at the School of Art and Design and we're leaving tonight to check it out."

"Wow, I-I-I am shocked."

Andy hops down from the table and walks around the store for what seems like hours. He finally stops in his tracks. "Why, why in the world would you leave the boutique? The dream you've built and the life you love? Sam, I just don't understand you."

"Andy, I didn't say we were moving to Savannah; we are going down to look at it."

Andy picks up his jacket and heads toward the door.

"Have a great weekend. Good luck with your decisions."

Not realizing I had locked the door he struggles to get it open and his frustration mounts. With urgency, I hurry to the door and pin myself against the doorknob.

"Andy, please don't leave like this. You asked me what was on my mind and I told you. I don't know what all of this means, but I do know that it's something that I have to deal with."

Andy puts his arms up against the door and I am overcome by his strong presence. Immediately, I feel protected and safe again. He leans down slowly and softly kisses my hair and forehead.

"Sam, I'll be here for you tomorrow, next year, next lifetime, but I don't want to lose you again."

I melt against the glass feeling the power and heat between us, but also sense the sincerity in everything he says. Andy reaches behind my back to unlock the door and sees a tear streaming down my face. He takes his finger and wipes the evidence of my pain.

"You're a tough gal, Sam, don't ever forget that."

"I'm not feeling so tough right now."

"But you're having feelings and dealing with them, which is more than you've done in years."

He slowly turns the door knob and I reluctantly move out of the way. I grab Andy's hand as he heads out of the door.

"Thank you. Thanks for not ever giving up on me."

He squeezes my hand three times – something we used to do years ago – and he is gone again.

I close the door, lock it again, and lean my head back on the wall. I feel completely consumed by the intensity and familiarity of our time together, but scared and unsure of the days to come. Realizing I have to get ready for my journey to Savannah, I gather my heart off the floor and head home.

Chapter 28

I take the long way home praying for rush hour traffic to magically appear at two in the afternoon. I need the extra time to compose my thoughts and feelings. By turning off the phone and radio, I am forced to be still and listen. Something I haven't really done since Gran's death.

What would Gran do in my situation? She modeled strength, but did that strength have rules? Lines that women couldn't cross or wouldn't dare cross? She always said to stand up for myself, but did that mean to have a voice that other people wouldn't understand or support? She always wanted me to be presentable and a "good girl," but how was "good girl" defined and who did the defining? Gran wasn't one to freely give answers. She wanted to see if I would come up with answers on my own which never seemed to be a problem. Now I am at a complete loss. How can I solve this when my mind and heart are at odds?

Almost missing my turn into the neighborhood, I abruptly come back to reality. Graham and Stella are building a fort out of fallen limbs in our yard. Graham has propped his pretend bow and arrow by the stick front door. Stella has gathered camellia blooms and scattered them along the thatch roof to show her feminine touch. Scarlet is soaking up the last ray of daylight while Myrtle is nearby pawing pine straw as if it's her attacker. I smile as I remember why I love springtime in the South.

"Mama, mama, did you know Kate is coming to take care of us while you and daddy go to Georgia?"

"Yes, sweetie, I did know that," I say giving her a big hug.

"How about you guys order a pizza and have a PJ party with Kate tonight?"

"Yaaaaaayyyyy!" Stella screams.

Feeling two hands grab my waist from the back, Matt kisses the bottom of my neck and for a moment, I picture Andy doing the same.

"Ooh, your shoulders are tense. Everything okay at work? Do

you feel comfortable leaving the boutique?"

"Yep, yep, everything is fine. I had to tie up loose ends for Carrie since she's working for me tomorrow." I quickly announce trying not to draw attention to myself. Is my confusion and guilt that obvious?

Trying not to leave a stone unturned, I rush to place the dozens of notes for Kate and the kids where I know they won't be missed. I show Graham the emergency first aid kit and take Stella to the back door to make sure she knows to keep it locked.

Matt welcomes Kate when she arrives, and my instruction to the kids iscomplete. They immediately lose interest in anything other than their time with the sitter. Matt puts our luggage in the car while I take a few minutes to cover things with Kate. I leave her money, numbers, Band-Aids, health insurance cards, and everything else possible to make her feel like I am the most overbearing mom in the world.

"You know I'll take great care of them. Right kids?"

"Rrrriiiiggghhhttt," the kids yell as if they've won the lottery.

Matt comes in to lure me out the door and we finish our ten hugs and kisses with the kids before heading south. As Matt moves to put the car into reverse, I unlatch my seatbelt and jump out of the car before it begins moving.

"Geez, Sam, are you trying to get killed? Where are you going? The kids are going to be fine."

"I know they will. I want to get Gran's journals to read on the trip. Please give me just one minute."

~

The car ride is quiet, much too quiet. It could be due to Matt's apprehension and excitement of what the weekend would bring. It's also undoubtedly affected by my intense afternoon with Andy. I lay my head against the window and replay the day.

Why do things have to be so damned complicated? I take a strand of hair that Andy kissed and put it to my lips. He had always been so tender, yet so strong. He knew just what to do and when to do it. Realizing I have to move past these thoughts, I pull out one of Gran's journals to read. I figure it is neutral reading material and could take my mind off of things.

Gran wrote in a daily journal each day of her adult life. The daily tidbits basically said the same thing: ate grapefruit and bran for breakfast, rode to the farm mid-morning, ate main meal at lunch, then went up to the "room where we sit" early tonight. Occasionally she would have extra commentary about needing more bran because she was constipated. Gran felt that her gastrointestinal health was as important as the health of her heart.

I spend the next hour reading excerpts both aloud and to myself. Matt and I chuckle at her entries. I can only imagine taking the time each day to write and never breaking the pattern. My heart aches as I read how happy she was when I would call or come to visit. Those were the highlights of her days. My favorite from 1999 reads:

April, 1999

Sam just called me and told me the news! She and Matt have a healthy baby boy. She ended up having a c-section and I pray to the good Lord that she did not have to struggle.

The little fella's name is Heath Graham and they're going to call him Graham. His weight is 8.5 pounds and he is almost 22 inches long! Sam says his hair is brown and he has a lot of it!

She sounds so happy. I know their joy and I pray for the health of Graham. To my one and only great-grandson, you have given me new life. I want to be healthy long enough to hold and love you.

The only regret I have is that I couldn't be there for the birth. I do know that Matt took good care of Sam and that she and Graham are in good hands. I hope to see their new little family soon.

What a blessed day this is – thanks be to God.

A tear rolls down my cheek as I imagine her writing these words. She felt such strong emotions in her heart and even when she didn't vocalize them, I now have something even more special. These words won't ever be forgotten.

With this highlight of my day, I easily fall asleep and wake up just as the car stops in front of a gorgeous home. In an instant, I know we're in Savannah as I see the moss hanging from ancient oak trees and wide front porches. These inviting porches are large enough for community gatherings, sweet tea, and key lime pie.

Matt rubs my shoulder as if he hasn't seen me in a while.

"Sorry I drifted off. I must have been really tired."

~

Dean Miller's home is like something I've only seen in *Southern*

Living. Its low country architecture style was stately in presence. The large front door opens and two adults appear, arm in arm, waiting for our arrival. They look almost dwarfed in size compared to the massive front porch and steep stairs leading up to the house.

The dean and his wife are exactly how I pictured them. They look like the poster children for informal elegance. The dean sports an argyle sweater vest with a pastel button-up oxford cloth, khakis, and Italian leather shoes. His wife looks like a sexy June Cleaver with her floral taffeta knee-length dress, and heels. Her hair is perfectly in place with a headband. Geez, I feel so underdressed and inadequate.

"Matt, so good to see you again. This must be your lovely wife, Sam." Dean Miller says while kissing my cheek.

"Hi, Dean Miller, it is so very nice to meet you," I say almost robotically.

"Please, please call me Dave. This lovely woman to my left is Caroline."

Perfect name for what appears to be a perfect woman. I feel as if we're in the midst of filming a 1950's black and white TV show.

"Caroline, it's a pleasure to meet you and we feel so honored that you have opened up your beautiful home to us for the weekend."

"The pleasure is all ours. All I've heard from Dave is how thrilled he is to have Matt consider this move so we want to do everything possible to help with that transition."

"Well, I do believe we're certainly headed in the right direction," Matt says as he kisses her cheek.

The home is perfect. Gorgeous fabrics, sumptuous bed linens, fresh food that would make Paula Deen Jealous, and hospitality that is fit for a queen and king.

For the next two days, Dave keeps Matt busy wooing him with the college environment. Caroline has me hopping with boutique shopping, lemonade and champagne spritzers, and deliciously sinful food. After finishing lunch in the historic district, I see an empty retail shop with a "For Lease" sign in the window.

"Oh wow, Caroline, this is a beautiful spot. I could have a second bridal boutique here in Savannah. The cobblestone alley is so quaint. It has great street frontage."

"I've got my cell phone. I'll call a realtor friend and see if she can let us in," Caroline says as she is already dialing her phone.

Her friend arrives within what seems like seconds. She looks as if she's walked right out of a salon. Her hair is perfect, legs are sun kissed, and she glides as she walks to greet me.

"Hi! You must be Sam. I am Caroline's friend, Tatum." Not surprised to hear another perfect name.

"Tatum, it is so nice to meet you. Thank you for meeting us on such short notice. My husband and I are here for the weekend and we happened upon this space that I think would be perfect for expanding my wedding boutique, *je t'aime*."

"No problem. It's my pleasure! This is a yummy spot. It used to be a children's boutique for more than fifty years and the owner died last year. She didn't have children who could take over the business."

As Tatum opens the door, I can't help but feel like I've gone back in time. The architecture along this little side street was the most charming setting I'd ever seen. I can add a trendy striped awning, give the front door a fresh coat of paint to make it pop, and do almost nothing inside as it needs hardly any work. The walls are a calming pale yellow that coordinates very well with the original heart pine floors. I would need to enlarge the dressing rooms since formal gowns can get cumbersome in a small fitting room, but that is manageable. The front counter is a gorgeous glass-front mahogany wood high-top bar. It would be perfect for displaying jewelry and other eye catching essentials.

Noticing I am mentally redecorating the space, Caroline gently lays her hand on my shoulder.

"What do you think, Sam?"

"I am very impressed. This is not why I came, but I feel as if it literally fell into my lap."

I begin sketching a layout on an old receipt in my pocketbook.

"You know, Sam, the sign says For Lease, but I do know that the space is for sale, too."

I hear Caroline on the phone talking to Dave and say they're heading over as they're done with their luncheon at the college. Boy, these folks do not waste any time down here in Georgia.

When Matt and Dave walk in, I can feel Matt's excitement over his day at the college. We spend a few minutes alone looking at the space and doing a bit of preliminary measuring. I ask Tatum about other bridal and formal wear businesses in the area and Caroline promises me she'll take me to them before we leave. Before I commit to another adventure, I want to know my competition.

Trying to be nonchalant in my excitement, I thank Tatum for her time and ask her for her business card. Tatum kisses each of my cheeks making me feel as if she's sure we're going to be fast friends and business partners.

Dave and Matt go back to the house to begin preparing dinner while Caroline and I peruse the local bridal store competition. One of the stores has no charm and is run by people who have none, either. Caroline knew the "Classy Bride" was no match. The next store was more my style. Its catchy name "Bridal Belle" showcases couture designers, but was still more like a chain store. My designers are both trendy and classic which makes the gowns timeless. The environment of *je t'aime* is feminine yet modern. We stop back by the rentable space and I snap a few pictures to take back with me.

"Caroline, thank you for taking the time to do this crazy searching this afternoon."

"I've enjoyed it. I looked *je t'aime* up on the web and I was certainly impressed with your boutique. I think it would be perfect here."

"Perhaps. It definitely gives me something to consider."

Caroline and I return back to the Cleaver house with a three course meal prepared by our husbands. We all laugh and drink wine well into the evening. It feels like a perfect utopia and makes me completely forget about my torn heart of hours earlier. Maybe a life tune-up is what we need. Matt would be happy pursuing his dream and I would be expanding my dream business.

Would it all fall into place? I would forget about Andy and how it feels to be with him and stop wondering again what a future would be like with him.

~

My mind begins to race about the new possibilities. Even with my adrenaline pumping, I fall asleep easily. Nothing but the sound of crickets and lightning bugs hitting the window screens. Savannah seems like a pretty great place so far.

Chapter 29

Matt is extremely affectionate as we wake ready to make our trek back to Raleigh. I feel certain his happiness is tied to the excitement he is feeling about our trip. He takes a shower while I lay in the Italian bed linens as long as I can.

My phone vibrates with a text message from Carrie who is caring for the boutique in my absence. "OMG-ANDY BROKE OFF WEDDING. HE CAME IN AND CANCELLED THE ORDER. HE WAS SO CONFIDENT IN HIS DECISION..."

My hands shake as I reread her text more than five times. I quickly text back, "Did he say anything to you about why? Did he say anything about me?"

Within seconds, Carrie's next texts reads, "Said he couldn't lie to himself anymore. Asked me if I had heard from you..."

"I don't know what to say. If you hear from him again, please don't tell him you told me. C U soon..."

With no time to process what just happened, I am barely able to breathe when Matt walks in. Trying to keep my emotions intact, I tell him my stomach is hurting and for him to tell Caroline and Dave that I'll be down in a bit. I close the bathroom door and decide to take a bath. I cannot remember the last time I have relaxed in a tub, but there is no time like the present.

My head rests perfectly along the rounded edge of the claw foot tub. I pull my hair up in a loose bun and let my body soak up the heat and the lavender soap. Everything about Andy has always seemed at arm's length until this morning. Even though we had reconnected, it was still on the outskirts of our lives. My family system was intact and his plans to get married were progressing. Now, his bold move to reconfigure his future was real. No more subtle hints and longing wishes.

My heart begins to race and my shortness of breath kicks in. I have never allowed myself to go there - to go with Andy - in my dreams. Our future has always been a thing of the past.

Matt knocks on the door and rescues me from the self-destructive day dreaming that would ruin life as we know it.

"Oh hey, honey, I'm coming right down. My stomach is feeling better and I think I can eat something."

"Sounds good. Glad you're feeling better. I'm going to pack our bags once you finish up. I'm eager to see the kids."

Ready to slip back into a comfortable existence, I say, "Me, too."

We say goodbye to Dave and Caroline and thank them profusely for their hospitality. I promise to be in touch with Caroline about the retail space as soon we make our final decision about moving, as if there is any question of Matt's intention to make Savannah his new home.

~

The quietness of the ride home is broken when Matt asks, "Sam, are you okay? You're awfully quiet? Was Savannah not what you expected?"

Realizing he is sensing my anxiousness, I latch on to his presumptions about my reactions to the trip. "I am fine, really. My stomach is still a little upset. That's all. I enjoyed Savannah, actually. I might just rest my head until we get home."

"That's great to hear. I mean, I'm sorry you still don't feel well, but I am glad to hear that the weekend was okay for you. I'll stop talking now so you can rest."

Matt is now completely satisfied and content with my explanation. He turns up the radio and I begin my internal struggle between right and wrong.

As we get closer to Raleigh, I text Kate to let her know we're close. Glad to see Kate, Graham and Stella throwing Frisbee outside on this beautiful Carolina warm day. Scarlet is sunning under the Bradford pear tree with Myrtle close in reach. The kids toss the Frisbee to Kate and run to open my door. These are the homecomings I love. It feels good to be missed and to miss them, too. Understandably, Kate is ready to go and have a few hours with her friends before the weekend concludes.

The kids catch us up on everything they did from the time we left to the second we got home. Kate let them stay up until eleven both nights and each morning began with pillow fights. Tired and happy kids are all I can ask for.

During our nighttime routine, the kids are eager for extra time with us. Out of the blue Stella asks, "Daddy, are we moving?"

"Sweetie, mommy and I are not sure yet. We're still trying

to figure it all out. I promise you that we won't leave you out of the details. We love you guys very much."

"I love you, too, mommy and daddy," Stella says in her sweet, gentle voice. She has always been an old soul. She can sense things are about to change but unsure of the how and when. She seems okay with the uncertainty, much unlike me who is churning inside.

The kids are finally settled in their beds as Matt and I unpack the last of our bags.

"Back to reality, tomorrow, huh?" Matt asks without really asking a question.

"Yep, real life, here we come." I say with a half-smile.

"When do you have to give the college your decision?" I ask even though I know his decision is unwavering.

"As soon as possible. I'd like to tell Dave by Wednesday."

"Ok, that's fair. That gives us a few days to process it all. Matt, I ended up having a great weekend."

"Sam, you don't know how much it means to me that you allowed yourself to be open minded about it all. I love you and our family so very much."

"Thanks. Being open minded was easier than I thought down there. Love you all, too. Goodnight."

Chapter 30

The next morning comes with a dose of "get your butt out of bed" as Graham runs into the room anxiously reminding me that it's Field Day.

"Neat! You guys are going to have a great day. I think it's going to be warm enough for the dunking booth."

"But Mom, you are coming, too, right?!"

"Oh, honey. I completely forgot with all the running around Daddy and I have been doing. Of course I'll be there for the morning shift – wouldn't miss it for the world."

I meant those words, too. However, I know there are a lot of loose ends at *je t'aime* that Carrie took care of the best she could over the weekend. I ask Matt to get the kids ready while I run to the store and hang a sign that alters the store hours from noon to six.

I remind Matt of sunscreen, water bottles, and beach towels for the events of the day. He grits his teeth as I recite the marching orders once more. As I pull up to the boutique, I realize that having options and choices is a blessing. The thought that I would be able to expand my business is truly a dream. I could take the property in Savannah and add a few surprises and twists to make it unique.

After making the quickest trip to Cameron Village in my life, I arrive twenty-three minutes later to see the kids waiting on the front porch step with towels in hand. Amazed that Matt has them ready and waiting, I feel sure he is trying to do everything he can to make my decision easier this week.

The kids are thrilled that our morning routine does not consist of the drive-thru line. Instead, we park in the visitor lot and I escort them to their classes and take my post at the water balloon station. My strength has never been tying balloons, but I quickly become a pro at the task after working with over three hundred balloons.

I watch kids play with no inhibitions for hours. No cares or worries in the world. Kids take risks to be dunked in water tanks and don't turn from water balloons hurled at them. I have the realization that a tendency of youth is not to hesitate and think of all the reasons why something should not happen. They jump in and take whatever consequences may happen after the fact. I can name every reason why we should not make a new home in Georgia, but why can't I make as many why we should go?

After I leave the school and send the wet and happy kids back to their teachers, I head back to *je t'aime* hoping to clear up some business matters and start making a list of reasons why we should go to Georgia to continue our life as a family.

~

"Thank goodness we're running again. I need it after gorging myself down in Savannah. I've missed you these last few days, Carrie."

"I missed you, too!"

"How was your date?"

"I am going to finally say his name out loud – I had a fabulous night with Brad. We had drinks and dinner at Midtown Bar 115 and then got coffee at Starbucks and talked outside by the fireplace until midnight."

"Did you all have a lot to talk about? Did it feel comfortable?"

"It felt really good to talk to a man about things other than business. I mean, Matt listens and cares, but he's like my brother. He even has his hair!"

"Will you guys go out again?"

"Actually, we spent Sunday at Duke Gardens. I packed a picnic lunch and we stayed curled up on a quilt until sunset."

"Girl, look at your smile! I'm so excited for you."

"Day by day, Sam, day by day."

"Yeah, I know that saying well."

We run hard but talk nonstop details of the Savannah trip and I get the intimate scoop on her weekend with Brad. Hoping to avoid a conversation about Andy, I keep conversation moving quickly. Thinking I had actually managed to evade talk of my situation, I say a quick goodbye and pull out my key to unlock *je t'aime*.

"Um, Sam, not so quick dear."

"Oh yeah, I'm sorry. We forgot to say love ya, mean it!"

"You try to be so slick, but I know you very well."

"Okay. Go ahead with the questions."

"Have you talked to him?"

"No, I haven't. Not feeling real comfortable saying, 'Hey, Andy, heard you broke up with that bimbo.' I figure he didn't tell me so I won't prod."

"No, what you're saying is that you'll sweep this into a tidy little trash pile and throw it out."

"I'm going to have to start having Kahlua in my coffee if my mornings don't improve."

"You know our jobs are to keep each other real. You know he told me about the wedding being called off because I would tell you while you were on your trip."

"Was he devastated when he told you?"

"Hell no. He never loved her."

"I just don't know what to say to him right now."

"Sam, I don't think he is going to come back. He told me he wasn't going to confuse you anymore. You have got to do some thinking because you actually have him back in your life now. You need to decide what role he is going to play."

"Why can't this just go away?" I say as a tear starts to drop down my cheek.

"Sweetie, you can't get rid of people and things that touch your heart. You guys held one another's hearts and it was neither of your desires not to have forever together. I believe both of you need to have closure in order to figure out what the future holds."

"You're right. I know you are. It just hurts. I don't believe finding Gran's letters was haphazard. I think that was her way of helping me heal long after she had the physical power to do so."

"You got it. Sam, just don't let all of this blow over. You only half faced it twenty years ago. Face the other half now."

I wipe another tear from my cheek and look at my best friend. She has a confidence about her this morning. A glow. Thank goodness she is brave enough to be a good friend and brave enough to share her love with me and brave enough to seek new love after many, many years.

"Okay. I've said my piece. So finally, love ya, mean it."

I watch her scoot away in her zippy convertible and try to get the courage to start my day.

~

D-Day, aka "Decision Day," comes quickly. Matt made his mind up about Savannah before we left Georgia while I have been desperately trying to make some decisions.

"Okay, it's Wednesday. I'm sure you don't have a clue that today's the big day."

"Why, Sam, I have no idea what you're talking about."

"After I get the kids to school how about we have breakfast and talk?"

"Works for me."

As the kids and I wait in the drive-thru line, I try and make some final decisions. What I realize is there is no one "right" decision. One of the things Gran always told me was that no hard decision is ever made without great thought and care. Boy, is she right. My job is to make my decision based on my family and my business without thoughts of what "could be" with Andy.

~

So used to using our BlackBerrys for our life calendar, I decide to take the printed one from the fridge. Living so close to the hub of shopping and eating, we actually decide to take advantage of our location and walk to our favorite brunch spot, Coquette.

For once not rushing to the next activity on our list, we enjoy the outdoors and people watching on the way to breakfast.

"You know, hon, I'd miss all of this. I feel like Raleigh is a part of me. It's a part of us. We're in the state capital, but I feel like we're in our own little community."

"We've been here a long time. I do think Savannah has a charming city life, too," Matt says in a convincing tone.

"Undoubtedly. We would be living in an almost iconic city."

We arrive at Coquette, order our coffees and pastries at one of the tables with the open veranda doors.

"You've made up your mind, right?" I ask, knowing the answer.

"Sweetie, my mind and my heart is us. Not just me. Yes, I would love to pursue adding professorship to my career. Would I do it at the cost of our family? No."

"I know what fulfilling your dreams is like. I do just that with *je t'aime* each and every day and it is so gratifying. You have been so happy the last few weeks since meeting Dave and contemplating this offer."

"I have, you're right."

"I want you to have that and I'm a true believer of people creating their own destinies. You've worked damn hard to have exposure with your art and it's paying off. My thing is I don't want us to give up either life."

"I can't leave Dave in limbo many more weeks. I need to tell him either way soon."

"I know that. What I'm saying is that we keep our house, boutique and life here but also include Savannah. I can definitely afford to get help at *je t'aime* on weekends and summers. You will have a lot of breaks with the college calendar when you can come home and stay. In between those times we'll travel back and forth."

"Are you saying we'll live separately?"

"Not as in separated. People do it all the time. It'll be like Savannah is our vacation home."

"I would miss you all terribly. I don't think it will work."

We both sit quietly watching life move quickly by outside the restaurant. It's almost as if we're watching all that is going on around us but unable to be a part of it. Like magic, I come up with what I believe is a great suggestion.

"How about asking Dave if you can teach Tuesdays through Thursdays so you can have four day weekends?"

"Go on, I'm listening."

"To begin, we could rent until Gran's estate settles and we figure out where in Savannah we'd actually want to buy."

"I recall Dave saying that there's a relocation allowance that could help defray some initial costs. I think he would go for the three day teaching week."

"As you know, summer is my busiest time at *je t'aime* and I couldn't leave the upcoming one to a newbie. Within the next year, though, we could slowly look at expanding the business to Savannah. I just don't want to rush in to that huge money commitment quite yet."

"I agree. It would give you time to learn the market and find people who could work when you are not there."

"Matt, I think this is all worth a try. If it doesn't work, we haven't lost much."

"To keep busy when you guys aren't in Savannah, I can keep up my painting. Will you be okay?"

Good question. I haven't even considered it until now.

"I think so. The kids will keep me busy during the week. In the quiet time I will need to get used to having quiet. It may be good for me."

We talk for another couple of hours. It feels so good to be open and honest about our needs and wants. It's been a long time that I stood up for what I wanted and seeing that the world still turns gives me peace about our decisions.

Matt takes the rest of the day to talk to Dave about the relocation stipend as well as the abbreviated schedule.

I open *je t'aime* and wrap up loose ends for the multiple upcoming weddings. Matt drops by with news of an ecstatic Dean Miller and we toast with a cup of coffee.

"It looks like we're going to try this after all. He'd like me to be there the second week of June before the second summer session starts."

"What about the schedule? Is it too late for him to alter it?"

"Nope. He was fine with it all. Since I'm having graduate level courses, he can make Mondays and Fridays open lab days in the studio."

"That's great, honey. They must really want you."

"Not as bad as I want you."

And just like that, we make love for the first time in *je t'aime*. He carries me to the back room where he pulls up my skirt and makes love to me with more passion that I've ever felt. His movements are strong and confident.

"Sorry it's so quick. I wish I could hold you for a while."

"Good God, Matt. Please don't apologize. I don't think we've ever made love quite like that before. We have an ongoing date in this exact spot every time you come home."

"You got it."

Matt hangs the "anniversary" painting and it is truly perfect in the boutique. I pray that one day I will not think of Andy when I look at the art.

Matt helps me finish up my tasks at *je t'aime* and we head home to see the kids. We decide to take them to their favorite pizza place, Milton's, to break the news of our new plans.

To our surprise, they seem settled with the idea. In Stella's words, we will be on "vacation" all the time. If that's how she wants to view it, that's okay by me. At home, we stay up playing cards until Stella falls asleep on the table.

"Well, I guess I won!" Graham says proudly and he heads off to bed.

"Sam, I have to say that if this afternoon is a preview of what it's going to be like when we see each other, I think it's going to work out just fine. I guess I need to begin getting things lined up in Savannah the next few days."

"Yeah, and I need to head to Fairfield before you leave so I can take care of a few more things."

"I had forgotten that you need to go back. Will you be okay to go by yourself?"

"I'll be fine. I was okay last time. I may need to spend a night next week."

"I'm here until mid-June. Since the kids will be out of school when I begin, maybe we can all go down and get me settled."

"Absolutely. You need my "decorating touch" anyway so we'll want to come," I tease.

"I feel really good about the decisions we made."

"I feel good that you weren't scared to tell me. Sam, we're going to make this work."

He's right. I said how I felt and didn't worry about feeling hurt or causing distress. God it feels good.

Chapter 31

In my preparation for my visit to Fairfield, I mentally and emotionally begin planning a pit stop in Greenville. It will be a perfect break on the way home. I haven't talked to Andy since before Matt and I left for Savannah and we certainly have not broached the subject of his breakup. I bundle a stack of Andy's letters to Gran with a pink bow and tuck them in my bag.

Matt's job is to keep the kids on their routine for two days. They'll enjoy the time with him, especially in the wake of the new plans. He and Jack will take turns covering *je t'aime*. Jack jumps at the chance to get his hands on pretty fabrics and since Carrie has a full-time job and a new boyfriend, Jack is a great substitute. He has no reservations leaving his shop as his new manager has turned out to not only be cute, but very reliable.

Still not giving in to my curiosity, I lay the note from Gran to Helen beside me on the seat as I drive to Hyde County. The drive is long and straight. I drink my coffee and crank Dave Matthews to help me stay awake.

As soon as I cross Fairfield's town line, my heart aches. This is the first time I've returned since burying Gran. I am overcome by a new wave of grief that I had not anticipated. I drive slowly pretending like Gran is telling me about the different people in the homes. I can hear her saying, "Maude just had hip replacement and Jessie lost his sister to a battle with cancer."

The thing is, each little house has a story and even though Gran knew the good, the bad, and the ugly, she cared deeply for everyone in her community. It's those strong roots that ground me each and every time I'm near.

The lodge looks good. We are having a neighbor cut the grass every other week so it stays somewhat tame. The gorgeous elm tree towers over the side yard. The swing hanging on the century-old limb moves ever so slightly in the wind as if it's waiting for me to jump on. It's a little eerie to me this time, especially without Scarlet and Myrtle. They always make a little noise which quickly fills an empty space.

Thankful that I put the plethora of food from the funeral in the freezer, I pull out several dishes so they'll thaw for my stay. My three items of business on this trip are meeting with the attorney to settle Gran's estate and paying my respects to both Helen and Gran. I decide to do the easy one first – meet with the lawyer.

I climb back into the car to drive to the nearest little town, Swan Quarter. The drive from Fairfield to Swan Quarter is visually stunning. With a few minutes to spare, I slow the car so I can relish the view of Mattamuskeet Lake. The ten minute drive over the lake on the two-lane road is breathtaking.The view changes each season as different waterfowl call the lake their home. Today, dozens of fishermen are hoping to get lucky with a cooler full of fish and crabs. A group of kayakers explore the perimeter of the lake with binoculars and cameras hung around their necks. I know my drive across the lake is coming to a close when I pass the entrance to the Wildlife Refuge. I chuckle out loud at the sight of two men fishing right beside a "NO FISHING" sign.

Now across the lake, the final leg of the scenic drive to Swan Quarter is almost complete. Queen Anne's lace and black-eyed Susan's line the ditch banks. Gran and her three siblings were raised in this area and I now understand why she never wanted to leave her home. The area is truly untouched by what I would call modern conveniences and Gran would call modern *in*conveniences. Many homes and spaces have been repurposed over time to preserve their architectural history and value. TheTunnell Farmhouse Bed and Breakfast is a prime example of this. Gran's brother and his family occupied the home which has now been converted to a bed and breakfast. A prime location for visitors hoping to hunt, bird watch, fish, or just need a stop on their way to the Ocracoke ferry, it stays busy year-round. I spent many a summer under the massive branches of the century-old oak trees. Dozens of historic homes that have stood strong for more than a century are sure to be around for another hundred years.

The attorney's office is located across from Providence Methodist Church. Known to most as "the Church moved by the Hand of God," this country church is no ordinary dwelling. For as long as I can remember, Gran would tell the story of how the church got its name to any new visitor to Hyde County. My most recent memory of this story telling occurred on our last family trip to Fairfield to see Gran before she died. Before we could set foot in her doorway, she asked us to drive her to Swan Quarter. The kids had been in the car for three hours straight and were ready to get out and stretch, but I could tell that Gran had a bee in her bonnet. Insisting we drive her car since it hadn't moved in weeks, we floated down the highway in her smooth riding Cadillac. Gran's memory had started to have gaps, but not on this day.

"Stella and Graham, I want to tell you about Oyster Creek Road. See this road we're on? It's the road where I grew up. It's also the road where your great-grandfather had a country store. It's also where God showed his love and care for this community. Matt, can you pull over to the church?" Gran was very clear with her communication. With no cars on the road for miles, Matt was able to slow down the Cadillac boat quickly.

"Children, this church was moved by God's hands," she says with conviction.

"Whoa, he must be strong!" Stella says with her eyes as large as saucers.

"Yes, honey, his arms can hold the world. Years before I was born, members of Providence Church wished to move to a new location; one that was safe from flooding when hurricanes came. In fact, they wanted to be right where we're parked. A stubborn man wouldn't sell the church this piece of land and it made the community sad. One night it rained and rained and the wind blew and blew. When people woke up the next morning, the church was gone! It was no longer in the low-lying land; it had moved to the land that the man wouldn't sell!"

"Gran, you mean it actually moved? That's not possible," Graham says with doubt.

"Yes, I mean it moved. With the amount of rain that fell that night, the church was lifted off its foundation and floated to its home here. It was moved by God's hands."

"God really wanted this church to have a new home, huh?" Stella says in a matter-of-fact tone.

"Yes, he did, honey," Gran said in a tender and longing tone. Our drive back to Fairfield that day was very quiet. That was our last visit to Fairfield before she died.

~

The only attorney in Swan Quarter, Mr. Sadler stays busy with all legal matters. I remember coming to the same office after Papa died. Greeting me at the door, I am startled by his obvious aging.

"Hello, Sam. It's great to see you."

"Hi Mr. Sadler, it's a pleasure to see you again, too."

"Dear, please call me Bruce. We're sure missing Mrs. Ada Grace around Hyde. It's just not the same."

"Thanks. I feel the same way, too."

I swallow big in order to fight back tears. We quickly get to business and within thirty minutes, Gran's will and life wishes are put to rest.

~

Relieved to know my cell phone strength is existent, I pick up a call from Matt.

"Hey, honey. Just checking on you."

"I'm fine. Long trip down but I just finished up with Mr. Sadler."

"Everything go okay?"

"It did. Nothing out of the ordinary. We've got to figure out what we're going to do with her house, if anything at all, but we've got time for that."

"Why not have a third home?" Matt suggests with a laugh.

"Yeah, right. I'm headed now to check on her house and then I'll be back at the lodge."

"Call me if you need me. Are you coming back tomorrow?"

"I'm planning on it. It'll probably be a little late, so just save dinner."

I can still hear Matt's excitement in his voice. I feel as if we're making the right move, at least for now.

Gran's house looks good, too. It's showing its age, but it should after nearly one hundred years. The emptiness of the house hits me like a ton of bricks. I can't bear to climb the winding stair case today; I want her to be here waiting for me and the kids, to have a roast cooking in the oven, and a glass of sweet tea with lemon on the counter. It's way too quiet and still.

Everything looks intact, for which I owe thanks to her neighbors. They look after the stoic home even when empty. I can see why it was so difficult for her to leave this community to spend time in Raleigh.

~

Before nightfall I decide to honor Gran's wish for Helen. Before I left, Jack had given me wildflower seeds to plant. Bless his heart; he does not miss a trick.

The existing blanket of flowers is so bright and prolific that I think I could see them even at midnight. Gran must have not missed one single year of plantings. What a magnificent tribute to her beloved daughter. Forgetting a shovel, I grab a kitchen spoon and dig in the rich black soil. It turns up so easily that I can literally dig with one hand.

Remembering Gran's wishes, I am supposed to plant the flowers and read her letter aloud. Whew, deep breaths. I can do this. I've already made the June 3rd condition so I can't turn back now. I carefully remove the dandelion clumps and place them in their new home.

Finally, I can unwrap the letter and read the words Gran wrote from her heart.

My precious Helen,

I have sent my beautiful Sam to read to you this year because I have joined you in the kingdom of the Lord. For decades I hoped and prayed that I would be able to hold you again and I pray to God that's what we're doing right now. If that is the case and I do believe in eternal life, we're both sitting on the oak tree's swing watching Sam celebrate your life.

What I know about life as I feel mine drawing to a close, is that I have learned from all the laughter, tear, pain, sadness, pleasure, and joy known to man and that for each of those, I am truly grateful. The sadness that I felt losing you could have been debilitating. Instead, I drew upon my inner strength to get through the days so I could live for my memories.

Now, it's about you, Sam, living for your memories and being strong. Sam, keep our memories alive. Do it with laughter. Do it with tears. Just don't forget who you are when you come face to face with the perils of life.

In your times of doubt, please take comfort in what comforted me until the day I died. I've always cherished the words of this Irish Blessing and I hope you'll do the same.

May the road rise to meet you, May the wind be always at your back, May the sun shine warm upon your face, May the rains fall soft upon your fields, And, until we meet again, May God hold you in the hollow of His hand.
~Anonymous

I sit with the note in my hands and weep. These are the last words I believe Gran ever wrote. She knew she was dying and wanted to leave me something to help me move on. Her strength and faith are overwhelmingly apparent. I always knew Gran was committed to living life to the fullest no matter what hand she was dealt, but I learned it mainly through observation. To read her words and picture her saying them makes her feel human to me again. She didn't have all the answers; she just knew the questions to ask.

~

The stillness of the lodge is not what I want tonight, but it's what I need. After saying goodnight to the kids and Matt, I pour a glass of wine and am thankful for the last-minute packing of Gran's journals. Her daily snippets have ended up being priceless words. What they have done is put words to her life. Often when she was quiet or stoic, it wasn't because she disapproved or didn't love me, she just wasn't comfortable with words. However, now reading what she wasn't able to vocalize, it makes me realize how important it is to say what I mean and mean what I say.

The journaling seemed to bring her inner peace. Each day she sought out quiet time to capture her day in words. Even though her voice was and still is felt in so many places, her true inner thoughts were shared mainly on paper. I don't want to die and have people wonder why I didn't share things with them. Carrie is right; I do bury things deep down into my soul.

One of the first things I'm going to do when I get back from Fairfield and before Matt moves is to start journaling. Writing down my thoughts and feelings will pull them out of their deep place within. If they're somewhere close to the surface maybe then I can retrieve them more easily.

I go to bed early tonight so I can get a good start for Greenville in the morning. I've also had enough of the quiet for one day. Baby steps, baby steps.

~

Knowing I won't be back to Fairfield until Matt is settled in Savannah, I take a few minutes to enjoy the serenity of the lodge. I pick several flowers, some blooming and a few with tender buds, and make my way to the Fairfield Cemetery.

The artificial flowers that line Gran's grave need a good

sprucing up, but for now I lay the blooms at the foot of the tombstone and recite the Irish Blessing that she shared with me. As soon as I repeat the line *may the wind be always at your back,* a gentle breeze blows the seeds from the over-bloomed flowers into the Carolina blue sky. At this moment, I feel a piece of my soul drift free like the seeds that will grow wherever they may land.

Chapter 32

Realizing that I need to quickly get used to quiet once Matt leaves, I drive without the radio and turn off my phone. I remember Gran's constant adage, "Be still and listen."

Since making the commute from Raleigh to Fairfield the last twenty plus years, I have always taken the bypass around Greenville. Today I'm taking the route towards what should by familiar territory, yet it's feeling scarily unfamiliar.

The streetscapes have changed along 14th Street. Many more dormitories line the once sparse campus greens. Even in early summer, students are bustling down the tree covered walkways. I pull into a metered parking spot and walk to Aycock Dorm. I could almost make the exact steps with my eyes closed. So many years ago I stood in front of the dorm anticipating becoming a woman and here I now stand as a woman, feeling like a child.

Not knowing whether Andy has begun his move to NC State, I walk towards the hall where he used to teach and hold an office. This is it - Classroom 213. Completely void of students, but full of emotion for my soul.

I picture Andy standing in front of eager students hanging on to his every word, his mind brilliant and his look boyishly adorable. It's no wonder he's done as well in academics as he has. I climb the shallow steps of the auditorium style room and sit in the back row, just as I did so many years before.

~

Completely lost in deep thought, I don't even notice a thin, pale figure standing beside me.

"Ma'am, ma'am."

I immediately look up and see a young man with thick glasses staring at me and calling me by a name he would call his mother.

"Oh, I'm sorry. I was just about to leave."

I guess he isn't threatened by my matronly, harmless look

so he quickly responds, "It's fine. Dr. Latimer sent me to pack up a couple of books from the desk and I didn't want to startle you."

Dr. Latimer. That's a name I have not heard in many years. Shit. He hasn't left yet or has he? Perhaps this young TA is going to mail his belongings.

"No, really. I was just leaving," I announce as I bend down to collect my belongings.

"Sam, Sam! Is that you?" Oh shit. That's an all too familiar voice. It can't be the squirrely TA's voice. I look up without saying a word. My heart beats so loudly it does the talking.

"Dr. Latimer. I was just about to get the last of your things together," the young man says with urgency.

"It's okay, Trey. I'll get them since I'm here. Thanks and I'll see you in the morning before I leave."

"Thanks, Dr. Latimer and nice meeting you, ma'am."

There it is again, the matronly name.

I make my way down the steps towards Andy and stop on the last one standing eye to eye with him.

"Sam, why are you here. Is everything okay?"

"Yes, all is fine. I have been in Fairfield and am on my way back home."

"Well, this is certainly a surprise," Andy says as he moves closer towards me.

"Andy, I have something to talk to you about"

"Okay, I'm listening." This time Andy takes a step back from me.

"You know, it's funny - I thought Gran was gone but I've realized that I have parts of her with me now that I never even knew. Not until recently did I know how she will continue to be a part of my life long after her death."

"Sam, you're not questioning her love for you, I hope. She was so proud of you. I see a lot of her in you. Her stubbornness, feistiness, and unwillingness to give up - you got those traits honestly."

"No, I do know all of those things. In her death, she's shown me how to live and let go of things to help me live life more freely."

Needing to break my gaze with Andy, I sit down at a desk and pull out the bundle of letters. I see Andy's face turn white as I untie the ribbon. I go to open one and he grabs it from my hands.

"Oh God, she saved these?"

"Andy, she saved each and every one of them. Gran kept these hidden with her most precious memories. I thought I had uncovered most everything when I cleaned out her home until I found two boxes that she had brought on her last trip to Raleigh. I just assumed they were more of the same I had been reading. I didn't take the time until recently to pull them out of a storage cabinet. One late night a few weeks ago when I felt like I needed her presence, I happened to find the boxes and began reading them. I had no idea, Andy."

Andy's hands began to shake.

"Andy, Gran cared for you, too. She kept these letters for a reason. She was the last person on earth to hoard junk which is how I know that she planned what I would find."

After a moment of staring off into the distance, Andy reaches for my hand and asks, "Why didn't you ever try and contact me or find out where I was?"

After a long pause, I think back to the confidence and strength I felt this morning when I was entrenched in my quiet place at the cemetery. I take a moment to center and muster the courage to be real and true.

"There is a reason and it seemed damn good at the time, but now I'm not so sure."

"Sam, I have no idea what you're talking about."

"Rewind back to the first Christmas you came back from Oxford, or well, Vienna. Do you remember the message you had from me when you got back to your dorm room after being gone to Austria?"

"Of course I do. I had no idea what it was about and I was paralyzed for months, no years after," Andy says with urgency.

"Well, after you left for Oxford that summer, I found out I was pregnant."

Andy stutters, "Pprregnant?"

"Yes, with your child. Our baby."

"Sam, why in the hell am I just now hearing all of this?"

"I was lost and confused for a couple of weeks and decided that I wanted to keep the baby. It was made by us and I couldn't bear getting rid of something that held us together at the time."

"Sam, I would have never wanted you to go through something like that alone. Did you decide to not have the baby?"

My body from head to toe begins to shake.

"I did know that. But I tried calling you and when I didn't hear back, I was scared to death and figured you didn't care. The only person that knew was Carrie. Gran didn't even know. I went to doctor's appointments and had started making plans for its arrival the next spring. One day in class I began to bleed and by the time I got to a doctor, there was no heartbeat. I lost the baby."

Andy holds my shoulders and looks me straight in the eyes. "You know that I did not know you called, right? I was out of communication for those few months only because it was out of my control. As soon as I could I came back to be with you and you were gone. You had left me."

With tears streaming down my face I yell at the top of my lungs, "If you hadn't have ever left, this would never have happened."

"Sam, I know. Damn, I know. You have got to realize that I missed you from the moment I left and it was truly one of the most difficult periods in my life. But, I also thought that we would reconnect over the Christmas break and we could continue building our life. Why didn't you ever tell me about this?"

And true to our every meeting, we are interrupted again. Not by anxious brides but by adoring students waiting for their last class with Dr. Latimer.

I scoop up my letters and belongings and run faster than I've run in years.

Chapter 33

In what should have taken an hour and twenty minutes, I drove the route from Greenville to Raleigh in less than an hour. Instead of cranking my normal rock playlist, I choose to meditate to Debussy's Clair de lune. I have finally done what I should have done years ago. It is only right that I shared with Andy what I had buried so deeply. Of course the conversation had absolutely no closure, but nothing he and I do ever does.

I easily move back into everyday life with Matt and the kids. Knowing our Savannah transition is quick on our heels, I try to focus on the inevitable timeline.

Jack took impeccable care of *je t'aime*, which I had no doubt would be the case, especially since he wanted to keep his hot new manager feeling needed. As a thank you gesture, I take him a cup of coffee. I spend a few minutes getting the scoop on new brides. On my leisurely stroll back to *je t'aime*, once again it's as if I am living a scene from Groundhog Day. There, sitting on the bench outside *je t'aime* is the man who has used the bench more than anyone else in the last five years, Andy.

"Hey. I was hoping you hadn't run away from life yesterday."

"No, not quite yet. I thought about it but then realized I would miss way too much shit. Plus I didn't have my running shoes on. "

"You're not kidding. Anyway, I hate that we were interrupted yesterday."

"It's fine. I showed up out of the blue which wasn't very fair to you. Besides, I've said my piece and I feel so much better."

"You're kidding, right? You feel better now so you're moving on? You cannot leave me hanging from yesterday. I still have no freaking idea why you never told me about this until now!"

Hearing Andy's tone escalate, I realize we need to go inside *je t'aime* for privacy.

"Look, Andy, I had to block it out. I had to move on with my life. The pain was too real and too great."

"Yeah, but we talked about everything. Why did you just let

this go so easily?"

"You have got to understand that during those couple of months, I was scared and literally catapulted into making decisions that I wasn't ready to make, at least not on my own. You were so far away and I had to rely on myself."

Andy gets up and stands at the window with his arms crossed for what seemed like hours. To break the silence, I ask why he continued writing Gran after I had gotten married.

"Sam, do you really have to ask me that?" Andy says as he turns back towards me, still with his arms crossed.

"I knew that I loved you and always would, and writing her kept me connected to you. About two years ago I went to visit Gran when she was in the hospital at Pitt Memorial. You had just left her room and I saw you, Matt and the kids walking down the corridor. The four of you looked so happy and at that point, I realized I needed to move on and make my own way."

"Gran never told me any of this. Why didn't she?"

"Don't blame her, Sam, it wasn't her place. Even if she had told you, you and I wouldn't be having this conversation right now. You would have pushed it all away again."

"So, why did you call off your wedding?"

"Sam, Anna is completely opposite from you. She's manipulative, trite, self-absorbed, and flighty. I was attracted to her because she is not you, but I realized that I am not the type of person who settles."

"Then why, why would you have possibly lived your life like that?"

"Sam, look in the mirror. Why are you living your life the way you are?"

"That is not for you to decide."

"It isn't, but I also know you very well and know that Matt is my opposite, too."

"Andy, I love you in a way that no one will ever understand. Right now, I am moving day by day because if I don't, I will push my soul so deeply inward that it will never come out. I also love Matt more than I ever thought possible. He and I have created the most precious thing in my life – our two children."

"Sam, I'm not asking you to make a rash decision."

"Then what are you asking? What do you want?"

"I just don't want to lose you again. Like I told you, I will take you however I can."

Andy wraps his arms around my neck and I feel safe again.

"I need you to know that Matt and I are going to try living

between Raleigh and Savannah. He's taking the professorship and I'm not ready to give up Raleigh and all that we've built here."

"How in the hell is that going to work for you?"

"We're not sure. We're going to spend weekends and holidays in the same city. It's important that we try this."

"It's important to him. But what's important to you, Sam?"

I pause and stare out the window. He kisses my forehead and leaves his lips resting on my skin.

"I have done a lot of soul searching lately which has been and will be a journey for me. What's important to me is that everyone has a chance at happiness. Matt deserves this chance at doing something he may love. He's a good man and a damn good father and partner in life."

A tear rolls down my cheek and before I know it, I can't stop crying. The tears are not from sadness but rather a release; a release that has been long coming.

"Why can't this arrangement work? The ideas of what's perfect and ideal are going to be redefined. If things don't work, we'll figure it out. Day by day, Andy. That's all I can do."

"Where do I fit in?"

Andy pulls me tight to his chest. My hands slowly move down to his jeans pockets where I can't bear to move them away. His hands move to my back and he holds me with such a tight grasp that our hearts almost beat as one.

"Andy, I-I-I."

"Sam, come on. It feels so right. It always has."

"Dammit, Andy. God knows we have a connection, and it feels better than it ever has."

"I know. We're making up for lost time now."

He kisses my neck, ears, and moves his hands up my shirt. They are warm and soft. The only thing I can hear is the sound of my heavy breath and his soft whispering in my ear.

Fighting the overwhelming desire to let my hands travel down his pants, I pull back as if I've had a bolt of electricity hit my heart.

"I want to do this but I can't. Not now."

Andy runs his hand through his hair. "Dammit, Sam, I've waited for you, for this, for a long time. I don't want to let you go again. I would never have left you if I had known that you were pregnant, that we were having a baby."

"Andy, I know and it's my fault for not searching you out during all of that. I buried it because it hurt so badly and I know that was wrong. That's why I'm trying to fix it all now."

My breathing is heavy and my chest feels like it's about to explode with hurt.

Andy just stares at me with sad, hurtful eyes. It's almost as if we have connected again. But this time it is because of shared hurt. The pain we both feel at this moment is like a bridge over time.

"Andy, I never wanted to hurt you. I know that you have a piece of me that no one will ever be able to take away."

"If I could rewrite the past I would, Samantha Lynne."

"But I don't want to forget our past either. I've realized it has shaped me into the woman I am today. The person who is better because of you and what we shared." My voice cracks and I soften my tone, trying to hold back my tears.

With neither of us wanting to look away, we stay locked in a gaze that we both know might be our last.

"Andy, I believe that even the hurt had its purpose. We got through it once, we can get through it again."

"Sam, will you please promise me just one thing?"

"What is it?"

"I can't make sure you're okay anymore with Gran gone. If you ever need me for anything, anything at all, you must know that I will always be an arm's length away."

We both see a car pull up and know our time is limited.

Andy reaches for my hand and pulls me close; our bodies touching with such intensity that the energy is nearly paralyzing.

Kissing my forehead before letting go Andy says, "Love you, kid."

With what feels like forty daggers in my heart I whisper, "Love you, too."

And of course, just like that, we have our very last interruption.

Chapter 34

My past walks out and disappears so quickly, I can barely digest what transpired. I'm quickly reminded of my duties at hand when the Edwards bride comes in with her attendants for a dress fitting. Trying to concentrate on the naïve bride and her bridesmaids, I'm fantasizing about when I can get the hell out of dodge and call it a day.

Finally after two hours of giggling and indecisiveness, the bridal party makes their choices and clears out. Not pausing for one second, I lock up and walk to get a coffee. Even though it is warm enough to fry an egg on the pavement, I need the comfort and warmth from the coffee.

I feel light for the first time in many years. After finally releasing the secret and confronting the man I will forever hold dear, I can fly and continue to grow wherever I may land. Until today, I had no clue as to how much I have been hurting by hiding. Gran often hid her words and only revealed them in her writing. Today, I have become my own woman.

~

I arrive home before the house is bustling. The quietness is a reflection of my soul. By trying to be so perfect, have I created this imperfect world? Nothing in life is perfect and I feel solace in this mantra for the first time in my life. Until these moments, I have not allowed myself to be human and have feelings. I sit alone, in peace, with Myrtle and Scarlet by my side thanking Gran for making me the woman I am and the woman I've just found. For long after she's gone, she will always be a part of me.

Scarlet's ears perk up and I know activity is on its way through the doors. Once again I fall back into place as mother and wife, knowing this is my position in life.

The four of us, plus a dog and a cat, begin our transition into the next chapter of our life. I do know, without a doubt, there will be both challenges and surprises. What I do with those and how I handle them is what yet remains to be seen.

Chapter 35

At night when I'm alone and working on finding peace, I walk through all of my memories, not just the ones that don't hurt, or ones that only "good girls" should have done. I am human, a real woman with real feelings and know that I am better for it all.

My journal has also become part of my solitude. Nightly, sometimes between showers and packing lunches, I make time to write the things I don't have to filter when I say them aloud. Tonight I curl up with a glass of Riesling and pick up my pen.

July 12, 2009

It's super hot here today – 103 with the heat index. Matt says it's blistering in Savannah, too. The kids spent the day with Carrie shadowing her for "bring your kids to work day." Even though she doesn't have kids of her own, Stella and Graham are the next closest thing. She and Brad brought the kids home tonight before going to an outdoor concert at Koka Booth Amphitheatre. They also brought me two quarts of homemade ice cream from Mapleview Farms. After a day of pseudo work and ice cream, the kids may want to live with Carrie!

We leave for Savannah tomorrow. This weekend we're taking the animals with us. It's the kids' idea, but if we're trying to acclimate everyone in the household to the apartment, we have to include Scarlet and Myrtle, too. I picked up four orders of Pad Khi Mao from Thaiphoon Bistro to take to Savannah for us to enjoy together. Hopefully the Asian-fusion comfort food will make us feel like we have a taste of home. I'm looking forward to getting away for the weekend and seeing Matt. He'll come here the next weekend.

Jack delivered a bouquet of the prettiest peonies I've ever seen. Like the last three Wednesdays before, the orders are paid with cash and no signature. Jack thinks I am trying to keep him in business, but I know that the person sending them would rather keep his name out of arm's reach. Even with Gran gone, I know someone is making sure I am okay.

One day when I am gone, I hope my journal writing will provide the same promise and confidence that Gran's words have given me. Life is not a straight and narrow path and I now see the curves and hills as pre-conditioning my heart for the challenges that are yet to be.

Sam

~

CPSIA information can be obtained at www.ICGtesting.com
Printed in the USA
LVOW132059300512

283852LV00006B/71/P